MW01703077

Reborn

Alpha's Claim Book Three

By

Addison Cain

©2016 by Blushing Books® and Addison Cain

All rights reserved.

No part of the book may be reproduced or transmitted in any form or by any means, electronic or mechanical, including photocopying, recording, or by any information storage and retrieval system, without permission in writing from the publisher.

Published by Blushing Books®,
a subsidiary of

ABCD Graphics and Design
977 Seminole Trail #233
Charlottesville, VA 22901

The trademark Blushing Books®
is registered in the US Patent and Trademark Office.

Addison Cain
Reborn

Cover Design by ABCD Graphics
EBook ISBN: 978-1-68259-940-2

This book is intended for *adults only*. Spanking and other sexual activities represented in this book are fantasies only, intended for adults. Nothing in this book should be interpreted as Blushing Books' or the author's advocating any non-consensual spanking activity or the spanking of minors.

For Tori,
I've never met you, but I love you.

Chapter 1

Collar of his coat flipped up to protect his neck from the growing cold of the halls, Shepherd returned at last from being called away by his soldiers. He found his mate nervous, the acrid scent of Omega fear spoiling the air. But, mostly she was expectant and blissfully unaware of just what was going on above ground.

And he would never tell her.

Shepherd made no move to approach the panicky woman, he simply stood as Claire looked him over from boots to skull. The Omega searched out any hint of what had called him from her, looking for blood splatter, or the swelling of his knuckles, relieved when she found nothing out of the ordinary.

His Claire was angry, but far more reassured that he'd returned seeming *normal*.

When the Omega stepped forward to touch him, to initiate what had to be done to seal their bargain, Shepherd spoke. "You are hungry, little one. We will eat first."

We will eat first?

Shepherd did not go to the door to fetch food. Instead, he went to where he stored his clothing and began pulling off his coat, armor, and boots. Bunched muscles flexed, he pulled his shirt over his head, handing it to her. Unthinkingly, Claire took it and put it, as he expected, in her nest.

Distracted by the task, the Omega chewed her lip, taking time to arrange the scented fabric and remove something old to be washed.

A knock sounded, Shepherd barked for the visitor to enter.

Jules came in with their food, set it down and left in seconds—the trivial familiarity he shared with Claire completely concealed by his indifference. She found it minorly amusing, especially the way Shepherd shifted to put his body between her and the Beta.

When the door closed, Claire found it very difficult to suppress a snort.

"What is funny?" the male growled, narrowing his eyes.

"*You* are funny, Shepherd." Claire arranged herself at the table. "That man has brought me meals dozens of times when you are not here—so you must trust him. Yet there you are, glaring at him as if he were not your friend. You have serious issues..."

Shepherd only grunted in answer. Dressed only in trousers, he came to the table. "It is a natural reaction for an Alpha to guard his Omega from dangerous men."

But not dangerous women...

Glancing at the food, Claire felt wholly disillusioned. She began to comprehend what was going on, what he had arranged for himself. This, the meal, was a show—a show where she was not spectator, but entertainer. She was expected to perform for the man lowering himself into the seat across from her. Reminding herself their agreement only required she initiate sex, nothing more, she picked up her fork and chose not to argue. Instead, Claire focused on the beautiful dinner, the male mirroring her movements and tasting the food.

It seemed awkward, the silence, and out of habit and good manners, Claire found herself wanting to make small talk, knowing it would be both pointless and something Shepherd would not respond to.

Except, he began it. "I have been told this is one of your chef's most famous dishes."

Cocking a brow, Claire looked up from the steamed fish and nodded, momentarily confused. "My chef? You do not eat his cooking?"

"Her cooking, and no."

That seemed strange. "What do you normally eat?"

"What my men eat. Communal food amongst those who've endured the Undercroft bears an importance I do not expect you to understand or submit to."

There were a great many things about the man she didn't understand.

Seeing that the woman was puzzled and still tense, Shepherd offered a modicum of explanation. “After years subsisting off mold, our digestive tracts have altered. *Followers’* diets must be bland, and the required nutritional additives have an unpleasant taste and smell. The bulk of my meal was consumed before I returned to you. This is… supplementary.”

Was that why he never ate in her presence? She looked at the beautifully arranged plate. “Well, considering all your other physical attributes, I think it’s only fair you have one restriction.”

The male smirked, gratified. “Physical attributes?”

“You are very tall,” Claire quipped flatly, taking another bite, not at all interested in padding the Alpha’s ego.

His foot bumped hers under the table. “List another attribute.”

Dodging Alpha pride was something Claire had years of experience with. “You are bald. It must save time not combing your hair.”

Narrowed eyes matched his agitated reply. “I shave my head.”

Claire sneered, pleased her slight had pricked him, and took another bite of dinner.

“You are playing with me, little one,” he added, intrigued, once he saw her mischievous expression.

Gesturing with her fork, Claire explained. “You’re arrogant enough. I am not going to feed that beast.”

Shepherd countered, his own evil smirk appearing. “You will later. When I move inside you tonight, you will hum about my prowess and strength… You will want to say all those things and more.”

The self-satisfied expression, the fact she knew what was coming—worse still, the fact he could inspire such a declaration—made Claire’s cheeks flame. She would cry out for him, admire him physically with her hands and tongue, but she would keep her words to herself. “We shall see.”

The grin that spread his scarred lips, the absolute hunger in his expression, only added to the Alpha’s excitement. “A challenge from the coy, little Omega...”

For a second, Claire believed he might reach across the table and devour her. Even the way Shepherd breathed as he watched her eat implied his exercise of control warred with his impulse to mount her.

“You seem like you are in an awfully good mood.” Claire thought back to how he had left her earlier, lingering anxiety matching the disapproval in her voice. “What did you do today?”

“Nothing of importance, aside from wondering what would be waiting for me in this room when I returned,” Shepherd purred, charmed by her attempted interrogation. “I think of you often when we are parted.”

Gods, even his scent was dripping sex.

The whole secret lies in confusing the enemy, so that he cannot fathom our real intent. -Sun Tzu

Sucking her lower lip into her mouth, Claire tried to figure out if he was trying to distract her, or mislead her. Looking at him, at the exposed musculature of his chest and arms, she found Shepherd sat with arrogance and authority, as if her regard were his due. Claire cocked her head, she tested. “If you were so eager for the remainder of our bargain, then why are we eating together?”

“Out of respect for my mate. I had fine food prepared and we are engaging in conversation, as you stated you desired... and as Dome culture dictates.”

Claire understood at once, this was not just a shared meal. It was Shepherd’s attempt at another courtship custom—like the foam flowers in her coffee. Pushing her hair behind her ear, her nervous blush deepened.

He exercised the softer expression he saved for the kill. Claire saw it, and knew at once her assessment was correct. Shepherd was, in his way, trying to woo her.

Unsure, Claire murmured, “This is to relax me.”

“Yes.”

“So I perform better for you?”

He gave her a long look that said yes, no, and a thousand other things. Unsmiling, his head just a tick to the side, Shepherd grunted. “You do not appreciate the effort?”

There was definitely a wrong answer, and that was the only one she wanted to blurt out. Biting her tongue, she looked at the shirtless man and said, “You are courting me.”

“According to your customs, yes.”

She was not sure what made her curious, but Claire had to ask, “Wouldn’t they also be your courtship customs?”

The man seemed momentarily at a loss for an easy answer. “There was no concept of courtship in the Undercroft. Men just took what they wanted. Violently.”

All too familiar anger bubbled under her skin, Claire aware that was exactly what he had done to her. “So that is the culture you choose to identify with?”

It seemed like such a simple question, but Shepherd took his time measuring his reply, as if tailoring it in his head first. “I choose to identify with military culture.”

The corner of her lips curled, Claire took another bite, wondering how on earth the crazy man across the table existed.

Shepherd disliked her reaction. “You find my answer unsatisfactory.”

Waving her fork, she stated blandly, "I find it unique. Very Shepherd-like."

"Explain."

Claire leaned forward and met his eyes with a harsh look in her own. "You have strong opinions on *my* culture, have made several claims of our failings and vices... but you do not have a culture of your own. Considering the aspersions you cast, it seems your personal experience with real society is negligible."

The male straightened in his chair. "I have extensively studied Dome life for many years. I lived above ground and below. I watched, learned, followed, and remembered."

The man was completely missing her point, or he was redirecting her on purpose. "Have you participated in *my* society before you tried to ruin it? Only watching doesn't count. Your military culture, the ethos you created for your Followers, is just Undercroft society tailored to conveniently meet your manifesto."

Shepherd warned, "We have our own traditions and an honorable philosophy, little one."

"That's right, a whole army of honorable monsters who probably roast humans on a spit for fun."

The man answered with a very droll, "We only do that on high holidays."

Claire almost choked when Shepherd actually make a joke. Coughing into her hand, chuckling despite herself, she found the male very pleased with himself for rousing her amusement.

She could feel the wheels in his mind turning, understood he had tried to banter in the same manner he'd witnessed between her and Maryanne. It was very strange to witness the way Shepherd's mind processed and adapted; he was like a sponge that absorbed interaction but didn't quite know how to apply it. So he practiced, usually falling short. Except that time... that time had been perfect.

Taking another bite so she could hide her smirk, Claire asked, "Enlighten me, Shepherd. Where do Omegas fit into military culture?"

Shepherd began to consider. It seemed like such a human gesture, the way he sucked his plump lower lip into his mouth, so totally normal, Claire could not look away. A moment later, Shepherd offered, "Napoleon was an Omega."

Claire blinked, cocked her head, and argued. "No he wasn't."

Shepherd grinned, he leaned closer. "It is a well-documented fact, little one. A fact pointedly removed from the Dome's retained version of history. Unlike you, I am not afraid to read forbidden books."

If such a thing were true, then why was it considered dangerous to know?

Claire did not believe him. “Are you telling me an Omega pillaged through Europe’s monarchies and created an empire?”

Self-righteous to the core, Shepherd nodded. “That is exactly what I am telling you.”

The idea he might be right, made Claire doubt herself. “Why would that knowledge be forbidden?”

“Because it did not fall into line with the Callas family’s crafted society all those living under the Dome are slave to.”

“Or maybe it was because that man was a megalomaniac and a monster. Napoleon was insane and not the best role model for Omegas.” Even as Claire disagreed, she didn’t support her own bad argument. It was obvious in her uncertain tone and disappointed expression.

“Napoleon’s rule, even his ultimate defeat, led to enlightenment, art, and the emancipation of the slaves in Britain. Napoleon changed the world through his violent actions and commitment. He was a very clever tactician devoted to his cause.” Shepherd offered what he perceived as a compliment. “Would such an outcome not please you, *little Napoleon*?”

Her soft breath conveyed trepidation. “Is this where you try to convince me he was a good man despite all the terrible things he did? That you are a good man?”

“No.”

Claire ran a hand through her hair, a nervous habit, and offered, "You could be a good man, Shepherd."

He leaned towards her, expression soft and voice natural. "We are not so different in the absoluteness of our dedication to change the world for the better. You gave up your very sense of self to the mob, reprimanding the city with your flyer—exposing who you were, trying to inspire. I do what must be done, because I am strong enough to do it, and I understand truly evil men in a way I pray you will never know. So you must grasp that I cannot be, in my duty, what *you* define as good—just as you could never safely live amongst Thólos society as Claire O'Donnell ever again. We both sacrificed our lives for the greater good."

She didn't know why she felt compelled to ask, but the question came before she could stop herself. "What was your reaction to my flyer?"

His entire expression darkened. "I was afraid for you, little one."

A cold chill, a creeping icy thing, scratched down Claire's spine. She was wise enough to grasp that for the Alpha, fear was something long ago conquered and not at all welcome. To know she'd inspired it was unnerving.

His grim honesty continued. "I desired very intensely to alleviate the pain displayed in your photograph. I was even impressed with how unfailingly brave you were to do such a thing, though I abhorred it."

Claire's attention went to her plate; she felt like weeping and didn't know why.

Her lack of words did not alter the undeniable tone in the thread. The connection was normalizing, vibrating, and creeping deeper. Before there might be anymore *courtship rituals*, before there might be a greater consequence, Claire stacked their cleared plates, ready to get her duty over with.

"Did you enjoy our meal?"

She nodded, even thanked him politely, hearing his instant purr when Shepherd's eyes flashed at her praise. The feel of his hand on her arm, the long stroke of light fingers, stopped her movement. She watched, stunned, as the man lifted her hand to his lips and tenderly kissed it.

Slightly hoarse, Claire admitted, "I am not entirely sure where I should begin."

He held her gaze, lightly flicked his tongue against her sensitive palm. "You could touch me."

The worst calamities that befall an army arise from hesitation. -Sun Tzu

Her entire strategy centered on action, on pushing boundaries between them, on growing stronger as she sought out his weaknesses. There could be no room for hesitation if she wanted to gain ground.

Resting a hip on the table, Claire did as he suggested. He wanted to be touched, so that's what she did. She traced his jaw and nose, ran her fingertips over his lips as he had done so often to her. Next, she stroked down the back of his neck, kneading the flesh he'd once claimed caused him pain.

Shepherd turned his head up to her, his mercurial eyes watching with such intensity Claire found her gaze rested far more comfortably on the Alpha's broad shoulders.

Keeping her mind separate from how familiar his body had become, Claire tried to approach it clinically, unsure if she was doing well. When a large hand came to rest on her hip, she took his touch as encouragement to continue. Her palms flowed over his arms from shoulder to wrist and back again, forming to the contours of honed muscle and absolute strength. She reached around his back to lightly scratch her nails over the broad expanse of flesh.

He liked that. His breath hitched, and Shepherd made little grunts and groans as she traced his spine.

When his purr grew husky, she rose from her perch and took his hand so he could stand from the chair and she could continue. With his great height, there was a shift in power, Shepherd suddenly so much taller.

Her uncertainty returned.

Timid, Claire's hands went to his belt.

Shepherd took her lowered chin, brought her face up so she might see the contented expression on his. "You are doing well."

His voice was gently encouraging, those expressive silver eyes liquid. Claire assumed he wanted her to continue, and licked her lips, trying to seek out the fastening of his pants. Fumbling, she pulled down his zipper and eased the fabric from his hips. Shepherd stepped out of his remaining clothes and stood naked under her touch.

When the Alpha made no move, Claire understood she was expected to continue.

Her hands found a path from his thighs, near his groin, and across the hard planes of his stomach. She nosed his chest, and pulled in his scent exactly as she once imagined she would do with the husband she'd hoped for all her life. Holding on to the comfort of that fantasy, she put the conjured image in Shepherd's place, and pressed closer, breathing in the smell of his excitement.

The fabricated man in her mind loved her, he honored her; he believed she was more than just an Omega.

It was so much easier to stroke and hum as her imagination unraveled, Claire didn't even hesitate to tease. Pretending he was hers, the mate she had dreamed of, she let it all go. Biting his chest, she playfully scratched near enough his groin that his cock twitched in expectation of attention—attention she denied, to instead reach around and caress his buttocks, relishing his groan of pleasured frustration.

By the time she closed her fist around his cock, touching it for the first time only to please him, Shepherd was already dripping, pulsing in her hand, and arching into her grip.

He wanted more, hands settling on her shoulders, he began to press her to her knees.

Claire knew he wanted her to take him in her mouth, a thing she'd only ever done in the heat of estrous. At first she resisted, a hiccup in her uncertain seduction. Eyes closed tight, hesitant, Claire counted to five before she could make herself obey.

Drawing in a deep breath, she acquiesced, kneeling to suck Shepherd's swollen crown between her lips.

The Alpha answered with a deep, rumbling groan.

Claire's hooded eyes dilated further at one taste, a dreamy hum expressing pleasure when more moisture dripped onto her tongue. Tangling his hands in her hair, gathering it from her face so he might watch, Shepherd relished her hollowed cheeks and the beauty of her pursed lips stretched beautifully around his cock.

Directing her movements, guiding her skull, with each bob of Claire's head, the male knew bliss.

She seemed so absolutely willing that he grew exceedingly excited, thrusting deeper between her lips, pulling her hair when that wicked little tongue swirled. Almost as soon as it began, he was on the brink of spilling into her pretty mouth.

His thrusts growing forceful, Claire gagged when he pressed too far, but did not fight back... she let him use her. When the Alpha reached down to cup his tightening sack, when he roared, Claire obediently swallowed around his girth and sucked harder for her prize.

Watching her little hands wrap around the forming knot to squeeze so it might feel like he was inside her, Shepherd spurt the first gush of semen down her throat, the male careful not to choke her on the copious fluid.

Claire gulped as much as she could, one stunned Alpha watching her effort, mesmerized by a stream of his seed oozing from the corners of her mouth.

Lost in the mating high, in her fantasy, Claire licked him clean, nuzzling into the broad palm settled on her cheek.

Shepherd's great thumb wiped up the spilled trickle running down her chin and pressed it back between her lips, the man groaning in approval when she eagerly lapped every last drop. "Look at me."

Claire, eyes black, hardly a trace of green surrounding the pupils, obeyed. She was so far gone, never had he seen her give in so completely. Seizing the opportunity, he pulled her to a stand, Shepherd taking her lips, kissing her and tasting himself in her mouth.

Even consumed as she was, Claire did not return the pressure.

Growling in frustration, he kissed her harder... but was penalized by the loss of her touch on his body.

Panting, aroused by the challenge and annoyed she continued to deny him her kiss, Shepherd changed tactics. The straps of her dress were flicked from her shoulders and the fabric tugged down. Breathing in her sweetness, biting and licking the valley between her breasts, Shepherd growled and offered in a voice rich with need, "Will you spread your legs for my mouth?"

Lost on another plane, Claire breathed, "Yes."

The Alpha reared and stalked forward, backing the little Omega towards the bed. "Do you desire my tongue?"

"I do."

He lightly shoved her down and fell upon his prey, his mouth everywhere but where she was wet and eager. Claire arched and writhed, exasperated to receive, but no touch came to ease the growing throb between her legs. Shepherd made her wait until he had marked her in featherlike bites, tasted every inch, until she was dripping slick from her enjoyment of his lips—the Alpha never having growled to call forth such a sweet scent.

Lifting her flushed body in the exact position to perfectly display her cunt, he pinned her. Her pussy was pink and throbbing, her hips wriggling against his hold, all the while her little hole twitching like a tiny sucking mouth.

Slick trickled out to tempt him, Shepherd flicking his tongue in the river of fluid, lost at only one taste. While he lapped up every drop, Claire moaned like a whore, rolling her hips to each flick of his tongue, grinding against his face when he burrowed that writhing muscle deep in her pussy.

With her mind still in that place she'd always imagined for herself, with her body in the hands of an expert Alpha she pretended might be the husband she once longed for, the feeling of a powerful climax swelled—something mindlessly perfect almost in her grasp.

Then Shepherd stopped, he stopped at the pivotal moment, and held her spread to watch her pink little pussy flutter as she tried to buck up to the mouth hovering warm above her. When she whined, his tongue stretched out and gave the lightest of licks, taunting her.

Fighting to move, to find relief from the coil of need he engorged with each darted swipe of his tongue, Claire's agitation turned to anger.

She had given him pleasure, and now her mate was contorting the vision, denying her the perfection of the dream by toying with her. Looking down between her spread thighs to glare at her tormentor, Claire aggressively growled.

The mass of muscle, the thing that was supposed to be fucking her with his tongue, prowled possessively over her body, negating her hips' movement each time Claire tried to rub against him for relief.

Brushing his wet lips over hers, Shepherd purred deeply. "Kiss me, little one, and I will give you great pleasure in any and every way you wish."

Wound up tight, instant wrath drove away all reason. Eager to punish for his attempt to claim something that was not his, to discipline for destroying the perfection of her dream, Claire pulled her lips back from her teeth. Nails scraped the hardness of sinew, her mouth attacking the bulging muscles between his shoulder and neck. In a rush, she pressed her teeth to his flesh and bit down with all the strength of her jaw, heard him catch his breath in surprise, and sunk her bite even deeper.

She wounded Shepherd with all the power of her indignation, all of the rage building up since she'd first looked at the behemoth, and the unfulfilled lust he had taught her body to crave and thought to use against her.

She didn't even want to fuck anymore; she just wanted him to bleed.

When the head of his cock skimmed between her folds, she dug in her claws and refused to let go. Shepherd penetrated her anyway, his warm lips at her ear where she could hear every gasped groan as he invaded her sopping cunt in erratic, desperate thrusts of his hips.

Shepherd began to speak, she refused to listen. He moaned out his name for her, she only growled like a rabid animal. He hit the place where her nerves were raw and need was everything, and that horribly powerful internal itch grew again, blossomed and divided her—blasting her into a sideways place where she had no name or purpose but to fuck and be fucked by her mate.

It was all there inside her, the raging storm that took away reason, it crashed and tore, and finally blissful expansion arrived.

Her teeth left the flesh she had deeply punctured, she swallowed the pooling blood in her mouth, and came as wildly as she'd grown feral. One more hard thrust, and the size of Shepherd's building knot grew impressive. It elongated her climax and tied the twitching thing to him where he could keep her still while his cock pumped her full of spurting streams, bathing her womb with soothing liquid heat.

The taste of blood was thick in her mouth, the red stuff under her fingernails, all ignored as her mind flew away in the intensity of her orgasm. Time seemed irrelevant, an endless field of grey... until a face distorted her vision. The beast whose heartbeat hammered against her red stained breasts asserted himself. Iron shaded eyes full of history and greatness, the silver of deceit and lust... those gunmetal disks looked at her with the devil's version of tenderness.

Full lips panted words, a rich musical voice undistorted by the rasp his scarred lips imposed, distracting her between kisses over her cheeks. "Little one, that was very pleasing. I am very, very pleased."

His mouth brushed her blood smeared lips, Shepherd looked deeply into hers, as if waiting for some act the female was supposed to offer. Claire lay there with his blood pooling on her chest and vague realization began to dawn. In horror, she grasped the consequences of her self-indulgent lack of control.

The depth of the bite... the placement...

In her fervor she had ripped claiming marks deeply into Shepherd's flesh, almost as savagely as he'd marked her.

The purring brute's forefinger traced over the blood on her lips, the trail that had leaked from the corner of her mouth, sniffing and panting and still deeply knotted. The warm heat of his tongue began to lick her clean of the red, bathing her mouth and neck, tending to a thing half in shock. The second his knot began to abate the smooth plunge of his cock began again, Shepherd knowing to fuck her immediately before her pupils contracted and his unexpected victory became her sorrow.

Making love to her until the Omega's exhaustion pulled her past consciousness, Shepherd did not allow her a moment of regret—not when everything was so perfect. Not when she was finally responding as the Gods intended.

Corday's head was in his hands, every last testament of violence he'd found stirring up a more horrible thirst than his worn out, simple desire for revenge. What he longed for in that moment, what he craved, were the whims of a violent psychopath.

He wanted to see Shepherd suffer. He wanted to watch him bleed.

Corday wanted to torment his rival himself until the sounds of the monster's screams might drown out the noise of the madness knocking about in his skull.

It was hard to swallow, even harder to admit there was no way to balance what he was with what a darker corner of his mind tempted him to become.

It was the room. It was the broken furniture. It was the blood.

The safe house where the Omegas recovered from the drug pushers' brothel, the place they had been promised, protection was ransacked. The two Beta enforcers set to watch the women lay dead on the ground, wracked with bullet wounds.

Nailed to the wall, his hand raised in a wave, drooped a headless body hung like a sick banner. The clothes Corday recognized, the stature, the smell not quite ruined by the stink of carnage.

Senator Kantor.

The leader of the resistance had been taken, tortured, and murdered, and it had been done right under their noses.

Shepherd was toying with all of them–laughing at them.

There was no sign of the few Omegas who'd called this place home. Though before they had been stolen, based on the stink of terror in the air, Corday imagined they had been forced to watch whatever had been done to a man he looked up to like a father.

"Are you going to say nothing?" Leslie stood at his side, staring forward, her lips bloodless, her expression dazed.

The safe house had failed the women it was set up to protect. The few remaining Enforcers, the stunted resistance, was failing the city they'd sworn to save. The one man unifying the flagging population had been butchered.

What was there to say?

Corday was crumbling no matter the stern look he kept locked on his face. There was nothing left.

Staring at the stump of mutilated neck, at the blood, and the open cavity of the man's torso, stepping over the entrails piled and stinking on the floor, Corday could find no worthy words for the corpse's niece. "We should take him down."

Leslie shook her head as if she couldn't bring herself to touch the abomination. "What do you suppose they've done with his head?"

He had no intention of answering a question they both, deep down, must know the answer to. Instead, he turned his attention to prying the body as gently as he could from the wall.

When it was done, what could be gathered was collected into the only receptacle they might find–garbage bags. Corday stood covered in his mentor's blood. "I am very sorry, Leslie, for agreeing to bring you here. He told me to keep you hidden, had I listened, I might have spared you this."

"You needed help carrying supplies. *I* needed to do something useful, for once. The months of my seclusion have shown us one truth, over and over. My uncle was wrong... I was wrong. My access to Shepherd's communications did nothing to further the resistance's cause." Leslie let the Beta see her need for vengeance. "The proof is on the wall before you."

Corday's response was automatic. "You have interpreted messages that have saved the lives of many of our brothers and sisters."

"How did they find him? How did no one know he was missing until this morning?" Face pinched, she whispered, "What if Shepherd... what if he only let us think we operated out of his influence?"

An ironic, painful chuckle escaped the Beta.

Rubbing her skull as if it ached, Leslie sighed. "Your visitor, that Maryanne woman, may have been right. If they found Senator Kantor, they know where the resistance gathers. Shepherd knows where you live. He knows about me and my access to this commutations network."

Exactly Corday's unspoken point; the resistance was in ruins.

Leslie had more to say. "What if your Omega Claire had made a deal with her mate? He may have been watching us this whole time." A question wracked with doubt trailed off, "How else could this...?"

He didn't want to hear it; Corday didn't even want to think it. "We must get back to headquarters. Brigadier Dane needs to be told what was done here."

Leslie Kantor grew vehement. "This has to end."

The word left him in a breath, he was at a loss. "How?"

"I have been to your meetings. I've spoken with my uncle! Brigadier Dane, Senator Kantor, refused to engage Shepherd's army. All they did, *all she will do*, is police the population and bribe potential recruits with food and false hope, while our enemy grows more powerful."

Everything Leslie was saying was true. Corday agreed with her, but the resistance was too undermanned. Weaponry was scarce, bullet stores diminishing by the day. Had they attacked months ago as Claire had suggested, a rebellion might have stood a chance. Now... the only prayer they had was to find the contagion and wait for the city to implode.

Senator Kantor had been trying to prevent such an outcome. He'd been trying to save as many lives as possible. He had tried to outthink a man far smarter than him.

Corday repeated himself, robotic and unable to even hint at what was going through his mind. "We need to take this body to headquarters."

Leslie softened her eyes and offered a sad smile. "No, darling Corday. There is no more time to hide away. I will not hand our city over to the inept hands of Brigadier Dane's failing leadership. There is another place we can go, a place my uncle refused to consider. Inside there might be food, supplies, guns, ammunition... everything we need to take a stand and end this."

Eyes bone dry in their sockets, feeling as if all life had been sucked from him, Corday made himself engage. He knew the very place she suggested and understood why it was off-limits. "During the breach, while my fellow Enforcers were trapped in the Judicial Sector, dying from plague, Callas's home went into lockdown. For all we know, the contagion was let loose behind that steel barricade. To force the gate could expose the population and kill us all."

She turned her back on the blood in the room, moving to the dwelling's small window and its slice of sunlight marking the ground. "There is another way inside, Corday, a small, secret entrance. Like my uncle, I know where it is."

The information did not surprise him. In fact, he, others in the resistance, had suspected there must be secondary access—an escape hatch in case of emergency. It had been Senator Kantor who fervently refused to risk the lives of millions to find out what might lie within the Premier's home.

Leslie answered his silence, turning her head to see him motionless, the corpse of her uncle wrapped in plastic and cradled in his arms. "If nothing is done we are going to die. The proof is in this room. Salvation might wait beyond Callas's door, and Shepherd would never suspect the resistance would gather there. Let him think he's won, that we've disbanded while we rally behind walls he cannot penetrate. This is our only chance, Corday."

There was another roadblock, the woman the resistance would look to for leadership. "Brigadier Dane will stand against you on this."

"That's why we are going to open it, you and I, before we go to her. When we come to the resistance, we come bearing hope, or we die as we should for our ineptness." She sounded so much like her uncle in that moment: imperious, confident. "Now, put him down. Leave my uncle here. He would not want us to waste time or endanger ourselves simply to cart his body to be gawked at by the people he loved."

He put the remains down on the room's only table, took a step back. Spinning the golden ring on his finger, twisting it around and around, Corday turned his furious attention to Leslie

Kantor. "If you are wrong, we will unleash the virus."

"That was my uncle's argument as well. Well here is mine: consider where Shepherd is from, how he thinks. The man created an army, still recruits to swell his numbers. He wants to rule, he has total control." Leslie's passionate words put a stop to Corday's endless spinning of the ring. "An animal like him would rather die fighting than submit to death by infection. Do you really think he would leave the virus lying around where it might be set loose to ruin all he has built? Even Judicial Sector, once exposed, was purified by incineration protocol. What virus infected those charred halls was destroyed the instant Shepherd's point was made. The people of Thólos saw the suffering, they saw the flames. But, we have not seen what happened in the Premier's Sector. Why? Why keep the population in the dark?"

She was as good an orator as her surname implied. Even shaken as he was, Corday could feel a small spark of lost hope threaten to chase away his despair. He wanted to believe she might be right.

"We can end this, Corday." The Alpha female edged closer, she offered her hand. "Come with me. Help me."

Possibility warred with the chance that obliteration might lay down the road Leslie would lead him. Something felt wrong, but life was wrong, the resistance had been wrong, and it was time to put his faith in something new.

The Beta took her offered palm and sealed the fate of the Dome.

Chapter 2

Shepherd ignored the blood drying on his skin, possessed no eagerness to clean the wound Claire's teeth had created. He left her claiming marks to crust and drip sluggishly, far more intrigued with discovering each crimson drop smeared on his mate—making a game of tracing them once she was spent and exhausted, tangled up in him and slumbering.

When they woke, reeking of sex, Shepherd made no move to bathe before he dressed, proudly displaying the scent of his injury and the smell of his mate on his body. Claire watched from the mess of the nest, a part of her itching to clean away the bloodied sheets and rebuild her burrow. Instead, she sat like a lightning struck tree, reeling from what she had done, awake and aware, and completely confused.

Her determination had backfired. Every part of her had wanted to bite him... no questions asked... even the parts poisoned with resentment for her mate.

Watching him dress, watching him watch her, it was clear whatever she had done in marking him came with consequences more severe than a beating or subjugation. It came with his apparent joy and her budding fear of herself.

How could she have let this happen?

Shepherd knelt before her, startling her from scattered thoughts when a warm, damp cloth was used to wipe her body clean. The complacent male purred for her. "There is no need to be upset by what you've done."

Unsettled, her voice moderate and full of lies, she agreed, "Of course not. I was angry and wanted to hurt you. That was the nearest place I could bite."

As if she had not spoken such an obvious fallacy, Shepherd continued. "Omegas rarely mark their mates. I am honored you did so."

The cloth was already stained, hardly doing more than smearing the mess on her chest into little swirls of pink. Aware Shepherd was focusing right over the bond, Claire could not determine if he was trying to soothe or gloat. A massive part of her wanted to slap his hands away and rage, to undo all her hard work with a monumental meltdown.

He who wishes to fight must first count the cost. –Sun Tzu

She suppressed the rage, the disgust and self-loathing, and embraced the fact that backsliding would be both stupid and pointless. Rubbing her eyes, giving herself a moment, Claire tried to come to terms with the new nature of the bond, unsure why she felt so vulnerable when nothing but reassurance was flowing through it.

Testing herself, Claire put her hand on his arm, cupping the bulge of muscle. Shepherd stilled and waited to see what the woman would do.

"I, um," a wave of burning anxiety made her stammer, "I didn't mean to bite you... I don't know what happened."

Setting the stained cloth aside, Shepherd's fingers burrowed against her scalp. He tugged gently and purred, did all the things which normally calmed her. "It was possessiveness, little one. I felt what was in you—the longing for devotion and happiness. You feel insecure in my affection, so you placed your mark where others will see."

Pulling the neck of his shirt aside, Claire inspected skin swollen and scabbed from her bite. "My motivation was not affection when I did this. I was angry, Shepherd. Furious."

"Yes, an assertive Omega disciplining her mate—reminding him of his place and duty... as I did when I bit you after you fled."

Unsure what to say, feeling uprooted, Claire grumbled. "If I wanted to discipline you, as you so rightfully deserve, I would have bit something else."

Reacting with no anger to her taunt, Shepherd urged her chin up. "You are nesting properly now, no longer ill, even content on occasion when you forget your self-imposed and unnecessary penitence. My attentive presence and our mutual effort has been the cause. You cannot tell me, little one, you have not noticed the adaptations I've made in my behavior towards your keeping. I will even admit many things are foreign and difficult for me to understand, but I do them to please you."

Verbal acknowledgment of his effort was odd, even more so, the man's admission he'd struggled. "Why make an effort now? Why not still treat me like your pet?"

Shepherd tensed, muscles flexing as if he'd been insulted. "I never treated you as a pet. I treated you as a mate, approaching the situation of our bond instinctually—as all Alphas do."

There was that word again. Looking back at the mark her teeth had left in his skin, she said, "Your *instincts* and my *instincts* say very different things."

His counter was so quick, it was clear he'd thought through the issue beforehand. "You do not follow your instincts, little one. You live entirely in your ideals. Therefore, I have researched the subject of pairings under the Dome and tried to adapt to what you anticipate as much as I can allow. I want you to be happy even if the circumstances are unfavorable and the goal requires massive effort."

There was something between the words, something she could not put her finger on. "You dislike the changes?"

"Many things suggested are unsafe for you."

Claire could not help but imagine a long list of horribly cheesy romantic interludes the man had probably read as if studying for war. Utterly sarcastic, Claire muttered under her breath, "Such as walks in moonlit gardens and dates to watch old films? Yes, those are indeed incredibly dangerous moments in life."

He didn't answer.

Claire looked at him as if he were something totally alien, seeing the man raised underground. Even crouched he was so damn big, looming, and too close. The male was playing the part of the attentive, well-meaning mate. That was not Shepherd, not the Shepherd she'd known—no matter the alterations, or the bite… or the suddenly wide-open connection between them he was waiting for her to acknowledge.

Before she just started crying in confusion, Claire dared an honest question. "Can I ask you something?"

Shepherd took her hand, enfolding their fingers—another thing he had recognized was important when communicating with his female. "You may."

Unsure where to begin, she blurted, "I cannot imagine you were so possessive..." She looked away for a moment in consideration. "That might not be the right word. *Obsessive* maybe." Starting again, making herself look him in the eye, Claire said, "I cannot imagine you were so obsessive with Svana. Her autonomy must have been respected. I also assume, and I am admitting this is an assumption, that you disregarded her negative behavior within the confines of your relationship quite easily. I saw how you looked at her..."

"What is the question?" Shepherd growled, not hiding his distaste for the direction of their conversation.

Claire rubbed her lips together and tried again. "Aside from the fact I am an Omega and you consider my dynamic inferior, why are we regarded so differently?"

Though muscles of his neck bunched, the man remained quiet, thinking. Speaking abstractly, Shepherd began, "I do not believe Omegas are inferior. I believe they are precious and delicate. Your purpose and roles are different, and thus your treatment must reflect that."

"Precious?" Claire's voice dropped dangerously low. Considering how he'd used Omegas in the past, she could hardly believe his gall.

Irritation flashed in Shepherd's narrowing eyes in instant reaction to her challenging tone. "You are very rare. Alphas vastly outnumber you."

Indignant, Claire pressed. "So you are telling me that because of your archaic view of social strata, you expected your Omega mate would respond well to a lifetime of imprisonment... based on instincts and your concept of preciousness?"

He took her chin, less a sweet gesture and more an act of dominance. "Your scent intoxicates all who breathe it. My Followers are well-trained and loyal... but animal impulse can cloud rational judgment. I will not risk your exposure to harm or tempt their lack of focus."

Claire knew better. "There are pills and soaps I am well acquainted with that mask Omega scent. Your argument is illogical. Intoxicates is also a very strong word that implies those around an Omega no longer need to claim personal responsibility for their actions. It reduces Alphas and Betas to animals."

"You should embrace your dynamic."

"No matter my feelings on my dynamic, you would still lock me in this room."

Shepherd countered. "You are my mate. It is my duty to protect you—even from yourself."

"Can you not see your behavior is extreme and unhealthy for us both?" Claire made herself hold his gaze, made herself still. "It is unreasonable and unnatural. So back to my original question you are so skillfully trying to evade. Why didn't you treat Svana in the same manner in which you treat me?"

"Svana is an Alpha."

Leading him to the words Claire knew he was avoiding, feeling there might be some small victory in this for her, she hounded further. “But you held her as your mate.”

“It is different.” Shepherd grew agitated, the male’s breath coming faster, swelling his great chest. “I will not risk you—”

“Me what?” One black brow arched. “Betraying you?”

“I regret allowing conversation!” Shepherd quickly reared to stand over her. “My answers will not please you, and you only seek to put tension between us because you are disappointed in yourself for marking me. I am fully aware of your motivation, Claire.”

Her point had been made—goading him further, even though she was very tempted, would be purposeless.

There is no instance of a country having benefited from prolonged warfare. –Sun Tzu

Claire had to agree. She and Shepherd had reached a point where fighting was not going to get them anywhere.

“I’m sorry… I just….” Claire let out a sigh, confessing something that cost her dearly in an effort to gain a stronger position. “I will admit I don’t really know how to process my marking you, and I am overwhelmed right now. Causing a quarrel was not my goal. You’ve made an effort. I know you have. I have questions. That is all.”

Shepherd exercised a chilling tone. “Your questions are incendiary.”

Claire used Shepherd's favorite argument against him. "Considering the history between us, that is inescapable, but *necessary* if you want to move forward."

"Fine. Then answer this." Shepherd's massive hand gripped her shoulder, assuring she could not scoot away. "What is it you found so appealing in the Beta? You touched him freely and were open with him. You were absolutely different with him than you are with me."

The question was an unexpected one. "You mean Corday?"

Shepherd's eyes narrowed dangerously. "Enforcer Samuel Corday, yes."

"First off, I did not even know his full name. Secondly, you are hurting my shoulder." Claire glanced down to where he grasped, Shepherd's hold lessening considerably at her complaint. "Thirdly, I hardly know him."

"Do not play games with me, little one."

Exasperated it needed to be spelled out, Claire blurted, "He's nice. The man had no agenda. He never tried to touch me or was sexually inappropriate. Corday respected my thoughts and wishes. He made me feel safe and unthreatened when I was very frightened and alone. He put himself at great risk and *actually helped* the Omegas..." Claire's voice dropped, the thread whirled, and something long unsaid slipped from her mouth. "The reason I originally came to you, if you had forgotten. Imagine how different our connection would be had you done the same—instead of weaving your mind games and constant manipulations. Instead of infidelity and threats!"

An animal roar, a thing of great violence ripped past the Alpha's lips. "Every last thing I have done, EVERYTHING, has been for your benefit—even knowing my actions cost me your favor. THAT IS WHAT A WORTHY ALPHA DOES FOR HIS MATE!"

Claire was struck speechless by the echo at his end of the link. Shepherd was not lying or hiding facts in justifications or outright deception. Whether or not she agreed with him, he believed every last word—passionately. In his mind, he offered repeated sacrifice for her and had gained nothing by it but the burden of her unhappiness and disdain. But there was so much more to his uncustomary outburst, layers of suppressed feeling that had to be difficult for a man like Shepherd to process—all there in the link, exposed where she could see.

Jaw dropped, Claire felt *everything* inside him.

Shepherd looked lost for a moment, the same expression he'd worn when he came to her in the bathroom after fucking Svana... when she had laughed at him.

His name came softly to her lips, Claire calling to him for a reason she did not understand. “Shepherd...”

His great paw seemed to hesitate, a resigned movement in lifting from her shoulder and moving to cup her face. Old habits die hard. He was already reaching for the zipper of his pants, but Claire’s small hands stopped him, and for once he did not brush them aside. She tugged on his arms, urging Shepherd down to the wreck of their nest.

Watching her with unconvinced wariness, Shepherd stiffly complied.

Arranging the male with gentle prodding, Claire placed herself on his chest, pulling the blankets over them both so they could lay still in the burrow and have the mutual solitude of the dark. He did not purr, not at first, instead she hummed her strange music for him.

He’d seen it with his own eyes. Leslie Kantor was right.

Access to the Premier’s Sector had not been a straightforward turn of a knob or a shifting bookcase hidden in the library of some neighboring house. In order to reach the second entrance, there was a series of tunnels, ladders—

an ant farm sandwiched above the Undercroft and below the city's foundation. From the look of them, those dusty, unused crawlspaces had been untouched for years.

Shepherd's men had not left boot prints in the dirt; they had not unsettled the cobwebs.

Was that because they knew the virus lay at the end of the path? Or, could it be that the tyrant did not know of this secret passage?

If Leslie was right, if what they hoped lay in wait, it almost seemed too good to be true.

The woman knew her way, though once or twice she'd paused and listened to the dark. Both of them had crouched silent as the grave, but noise could be heard: the whining of buried pipes, the distant clank of metal. Not once did she seem unsure, but she was extremely cautious.

The crawl took less than an hour, though every passing minute felt like a lifetime.

One final turn in the path, and a pressurized door adorned with a crank wheel waited. The design was clever, one that would not be affected by electricity, or a lack thereof. The Callas family had exercised caution in the design of their home.

Not that it had saved them...

Between the two of them, the Beta straining and an Alpha small for her dynamic, they barely had the strength to turn the rusted crank. One would think it had been decades since a soul had used this passage by the way the gears stuck. It took the pair longer to unhinge that door than it had to manage the difficult path to it.

On the other side, once the portal swung in, waited more darkness, more dust, and stale air. When they stepped over that threshold, Leslie suggested they seal their entrance, whispering that should she be wrong, the airborne virus would have little chance to escape and potentially infect the population.

It seemed even darker on the other side of that terrifying door.

A shoddy flashlight between them, Leslie and Corday were forced to press themselves together in the confined space; both inhaled and exhaled air that might kill them. After ten ordinary minutes, Corday actually smiled.

Leslie smiled right back, reaching forward to embrace him in their triumph.

His clothing was still stained from his encounter with Senator Kantor's corpse, he smelled vile and was laden with dust, but she didn't seem to care. Leslie pressed closer, thanked him in repeated sweet whispers at his ear.

He could not help but hug her back. "Let's remain vigilant. We still don't know what waits inside."

Enthusiastically, she pressed a kiss to his cheek, a happy tear running through the dirt on her own. "But there is no virus here. We'd both be coughing by now if there were."

It was a victory Corday sorely needed.

The deeper they got into the mansion, with its private gardens and warmth, the more they realized this segment of the Dome was still intact. There were no cracks, no ice. Trees in the atriums bore fruit in the environment's false summer.

Surrounded by thriving plant life, Corday reached for an orange, stared at the overripe fruit's dimpled peel. At his feet were its rotting brothers, each one having been wasted with no one to tend the garden or gather the produce. In those fallen fruit, he saw a parody of the resistance, the waste of lost souls, and the foolishness of almost a year of inaction.

How many good men and women had died while Senator Kantor had been extolling caution?

They had only grown weaker...

Leslie claimed he'd known of this place. Why had the old man been so afraid of a door he must have recognized would not have led to the infection of civilians... not when it was underground and difficult to approach. Teams could have been sent, communication via radio established, and a cave-in organized should the volunteers fall ill with infection.

Walking through those silent, elegantly appointed rooms, Corday begin to feel the stirrings of anger towards the old man. Why had he been so afraid of this place?

Claire was also there in his thoughts, her timid smile and faith. How much more had she suffered because Senator Kantor had refused to open a single door?

Room by room, hall by hall, Corday and Leslie found more than fruit.

There were decomposed bodies that had sat so long in the heat, they had putrefied, then mummified. The elite Enforcer guard of the Premier, every last one of them lay dead. But, it was the way they had died that was most unnerving.

No virus had been there.

Not a single guard had drawn their weapons. Yet, many had broken necks, their heads completely turned around—as if one by one, a shadow had crept up upon them and laid them to waste.

Corday did not see one gunshot victim. This carnage had been done with bare hands.

The deeper they moved, the more obvious it became. Something very wrong had taken place here.

Shepherd, his Followers, had done this, and then they had shut it up.

Why?

Why seal up the Premier's Sector? Why not make use of the arms, the food, the space, the warmth? Under the Dome, even Shepherd's soldiers were suffering from the cold.

They found what might be an answer in the most prominent room in the mansion. With a view overlooking the icy mountains in the distance, sat a desk, a flag every citizen of Thólos had seen via COMscreen during Premier Callas mandatory weekly address to the population behind it. There was not a wall, a piece of furniture, or even a window that was not grimy with old, crusted blood spatter. What was left of Callas body was in pieces scattered all over the floor. Fingers, parts of an arm, segments of leg... his limbs had been splintered, ripped from his torso, and flung about. Even the ceiling held traces of mushed organs stuck to it.

Shriveled up innards coated the floor, lay tossed aside in the corners, the broken, splintered edges of exposed bone a testament to the rage of his killer.

Not two hours prior, Corday had imagined committing this very type of violence against Shepherd. Seeing it in person was extremely sobering.

He could not do this to another person...not even the man who'd murdered his people.

Leslie went to her knees near the fragmented and crushed skull of the man she claimed was preparing to make her his bride. "I knew he was dead, but this..."

Corday had watched her when her eyes roved over the scene in the safe house, seen how she'd looked at the lifeless body of her uncle... as if she didn't understand what she saw. Her face had been blank, her eyes blinking slowly. Never had she cried.

It had been the shock, he was sure.

Now, there were tears on her face.

Corday watched Leslie grieve over a man who had been one of the first true casualties of the breach, and wondered at the difference between her impassive, determined reaction to her uncle's body and her silent tears seeing the old remains of the man she'd loved, ripped to shreds.

Something seemed strange in the behavior.

A loving uncle who had secreted her away so that even the resistance might not harm her, and Leslie Kantor would not even help in removing his body from the wall it was nailed to. Now this, her open weeping over a man she admittedly accepted as long dead, her fingertips tracing the sharp edges of his cracked skull.

"You must have loved him very much." Corday took a deep breath and let a sigh past his lips. "After you left your parent's safe room, why did you not come here first?"

Open apology in her wide china blue eyes, Leslie admitted, "I tried to. I could not turn the crank on the door with my strength alone."

There had not been a single set of footprints in the corridor's dust. If she had tried a few months ago, then the accumulating grime would have shown some trace of her tracks. She was lying.

Corday was unsure if it mattered, so he nodded as if he understood. “Of course.”

Hand to her knee, Leslie abandoned the bones of Premier Callas, and pressed her body to stand. “We found what we came for. Now, you and I must draw the resistance here.”

It was not going to be quite that simple. If they had been infiltrated, then Corday understood it would be an easy thing for Shepherd to learn of this new place. “If your plan is going to work, Shepherd cannot be allowed to believe the resistance perseveres. We have to let him believe we’ve given up.”

“Agreed.” Wiping her hands on her pants, Leslie offered a sad smile. “We must make him think we’ve failed. Let Shepherd believe the murder of my uncle broke our lines. The resistance as it is today will fade away. A new rebellion will rise up in the shadows where our oppressor cannot see. He’ll never even know we were here.”

Looking out her window, Claire tried to focus on distant snow covered peaks. But there was a much brighter, far more tempting view sitting behind her. Fingertips cold on the glass, thread warm in her chest, she felt pulled in two directions.

The familiar rasp purred, "You are thinking of my shoulder. You wonder if I am in pain. Would you like to see it?"

She always wanted to see the place where she'd bit him, could hardly suppress the need to touch her fresh mark when he was near. But Claire didn't answer, aware he was trying to tempt her from the view.

Her anxiety spiked with the understanding of how easily he could do it. Shepherd's purr heightened, she calmed.

Rolling her neck, letting out a sigh, Claire gazed at nature. How ironic considering nature was twisting up her insides.

Drumming her fingers against the glass, debating available courses of action, Claire kept her eyes off the male.

When the enemy is relaxed, make them toil. When full, starve them. When settled, make them move. –Sun Tzu

The directive seemed simple enough, but over the last week, Claire kept catching herself enacting the opposite effect on Shepherd.

He was already toiling and weary; her presence relaxed him. The Alpha was starved for affection, so hungry for it he soaked it up like a man who had never known such a thing—greedy for any scrap at all. A soft pet here—Claire looking down to find her hand on him, unsure when or how it got there. A gentle smile there—her expression relaxed without her knowledge or intent. And all it seemed the Alpha wanted was to settle and be still with her.

She was slipping, failing, her resistance having been crushed by her own strategy to know him… or offered up to advance it. She was not sure which.

Perspective, to seek out her enemy's weaknesses, that had been her goal. Having marked him and the subsequent blossoming of the link left Claire with a view so undiluted, no other person would ever see her Alpha as she could. Mission achieved.

She *knew* Shepherd.

What she found inside the man was so inundated in his makeup, she wondered if he even understood what it was—loneliness, emptiness calling for her to fill it.

When she mustered the courage to look, Claire could see his perceived selflessness. Shepherd wanted the world to be good because he had never known good, he had never lived it, and he could not fathom it outside of books and study. All Shepherd knew was that *good* was the opposite of the Undercroft, and that *bad* had to suffer in order for change to bloom.

He purred behind her. “Do not frown, little one.”

Seeing him past the hubris made it so very hard to resist giving him exactly what he wanted, especially when faced with the eagerness in which he offered himself and openly admired what he saw in her. Unless she stopped and drew back, unless she gave up her mission to open his eyes, she was going to feel... more than empathy or compassion.

Maybe she already did.

Claire had worried over it, fallen into brooding silences, and found herself more than once asking for the room with the window where she could seek distraction. Shepherd tended to comply with her vocalized desires, would sit with her as Claire did as she pleased—played the piano, stared out over her vast snowy landscape, painted in the sunlight—whatever she wanted. And he would remain attentive and watchful, his side of the bond wide open, Shepherd practically yanking on the link to draw her emotionally nearer.

He was the one making her toil, making her starve, and making her move. And all he had to do was sit there and wait as her own nature worked on her.

It wasn’t fair.

“Shepherd,” Claire said, turning mournful eyes away from the glass to glance at him over her shoulder. “I am tired.”

He knew she was not referring to physical exhaustion. “I know you are.”

“I’m not very good at this.”

“You are improving daily.”

She sighed, partially unconcerned they were discussing their long running personal war as if it were openly acknowledged between them. “Are you tired, Shepherd?”

Lounging back in the comfortable chair like a king on his throne, he shook his head. “No. I am the opposite.”

Narrowing her eyes, Claire fought the overwhelming urge to kick him in the shin. Feeling the need to knock him down a peg, she coolly reminded, “On the ice, I told you an apology would not make any difference.” Squaring to face him, feeling something unpleasant surge in her gut, she tried to make him toil, starve, and move. “I want one now.”

He was somewhat surprised, slowly standing from his chair, towering over her.

When it seemed he was only going to loom, Claire chose to walk away, but Shepherd began to lower and the anger all but fell off her face.

He got on his knees.

They were almost eye to eye when Shepherd said, “Claire O’Donnell, I am sorry.”

“Gods dammit,” Clare snarled under her breath, moving past him to flop back into the oversized chair, confident she'd lost another battle.

Swiveling, he faced her and leaned over, caging her with his arms. "Did I not grovel properly?"

A slight tick came to the corner of her lips. "Would you have knelt on the ice?"

He shifted enough that his torso parted her knees. Shepherd smiled at her while he warned wickedly, "Little one, you are in my chair."

"What happened to the whole Shepherd philosophy of take what you want? I wanted it, I took it. It's my chair now," Claire quipped. A second later, she realized she was practically flirting.

Confusion weakened her smirk.

Shepherd started purring, his big hands kneading the muscles atop her thighs.

Closing her eyes and leaning back, Claire let out a shaky breath. "Maryanne was right. I have it better than everyone else in Thólos. I am kept warm. I eat great food. You have created an alternate reality for me filled with distractions, including time with my friend whom I know you dislike, and pictures of the people I care about so I won't worry over them."

Shepherd grunted. "You did not make a point in your statement."

Dark lashes lifted and Claire looked at the man whose face hovered so near her own. "Do you have any idea how hard it is for an Omega to ignore the call of her Alpha? It's torture. It physically makes one feel as if their skin is peeling off. Then there is the fear, not only of the searching mate but of oneself. You hear things... there are tactile hallucinations. Your mind rebels against your wishes. You become powerless."

Heartbreak lay in her eyes. "The first time I escaped I would have sworn you were watching me from every shadow. I woke screaming each night. Every time you weren't there, I felt betrayed, even though I had run from you. My second lapse of freedom, I wandered Thólos and felt nothing. There was no pain, there were no dreams. I was empty—that in its own way was hell. But, day in and day out, I was searching for something, and every day I would get a little closer to the Citadel." Claire shook her head as the truth had only just dawned on her. "I did not even realize that until now."

Shepherd's eyes were glowing as he soaked in every word like it was vital, so still it would have frightened her in the early days.

Claire touched a slightly puckered scar on his cheek. "I cannot paint this expression. That right there is the enigma, isn't it?"

Shepherd wrapped his arms around her waist, pulling her to the end of the seat so their bodies could be flush. "Tell me more, little one. I want to hear more."

There was one more thing she could say that would affect him.

"I can't live like this." She studied his eyes, trying to capture the image in her mind. "I need to go outside. I need to taste fresh air."

"No." Shepherd let her go, stood, and moved away, dismissing the conversation, leaving her disappointed and awkward.

Already pulling out the handcuff, he waited near the door, silently signaling their time in the room was at an end.

"I give you my word I won't try to escape," she offered softly, seeing his head fractionally turn her way at the confession. "There are too many lives at stake."

Cocking his head, he asked, "Is that the only reason you would stay?"

All warfare is based on deception. –Sun Tzu

Fisting her hands in her skirt, Claire stood and went to him so he might chain her. "No, it's not the only reason."

Shepherd watched her hold out her wrist for him, the man reached out a hand to ever so softly run the back of his fingers over her delicate skin.

While she stood obediently, he spoke again, pocketing the handcuff and leaving her arm free. "You are asking for my trust when you have not earned it."

Claire did not so much as blink an eye. "You ask me for the same thing daily."

Chapter 3

His Omega's cheeks were pink and lovely from her exertion trying to match his larger steps, but it was the flatness of her eyes Shepherd did not like. They turned another corner, walking down the hall that led to his quarters, no soul in sight, as he had ordered all his men to vacate the halls so his Omega would be left alone.

There was no handcuff between them, an act Shepherd felt deserved a great reward, but Claire seemed to not recognize his generosity on the topic. She'd hardly even looked around, not that there was much to see.

She was so unhappy...

His mate reminded him of a fish in a bowl, staring vacantly at a world she would never be able to breathe in. It was clear from her end of the link that there was no pleasure in it for her, that the walk was unwelcome—that she felt more trapped without the chain than she had felt for weeks locked away in his den.

He wondered if she was punishing herself again, if that was what made her cling to his arm when she was miserable. Or, if it was some test. Shepherd did not ask. Instead he stayed close, looking over his domain, measuring what might be a threat, what waited around every corner, observing those stark halls in a tactical way she never could.

But this walk was not working. He pulled her another direction, and punched a code into a steel door. It opened, and though there was no sky or view, icy wind blasted their way.

The armed soldiers at the portal kept their heads forward once they realized who'd come. Claire went to step out, to pass through the tunnel to see where the breeze was coming from.

Shepherd did not allow her move. "I cannot guarantee your safety outside right now, little one. Breath your air, feel the cold, enjoy what you can before I must return you to our nest."

She had not expected him to even partially concede to her request, not after feeling the swell of unease that rolled through the male when she'd told him she needed to go outside. Shepherd was too determined to keep her quarantined underground.

Leaning as far forward as his great arm would allow, Claire had a slender glimpse of a city blown away on the wind, all of her ideals made into some mockery with the stink of dead bodies, of smoke wafting her way. Thólos had grown so much harder to comprehend. A part of her had begun to resent it, and at moments like those—moments when Shepherd's feelings somehow mingled with hers—Claire struggled to remind herself that she loved the city she could barely glimpse down the passageway.

Abiding disgust for what she'd seen, run from, feared... not all of it was Shepherd's influence. It came from her.

It shamed her.

Her memories of happier times were growing tarnished. She was finding flaws in them—almost as if Shepherd were whispering in her ear the darker things she'd endured and refused to acknowledge. Thólos had been dangerous her whole life. She'd hardly felt safe walking the street alone, even in broad daylight... because the city had teeth and claws.

No one had talked about it, but Omegas out in the open had always been snatched up by predators. Thólos's rich and powerful... the ones who made the rules… taking without permission, pretending it was all civilized, all acceptable. After all, who on earth had the power to stand up to the Senators, the Enforcers, the Judges?

Shepherd was right. She had never once been free.

Even in civilized Thólos, her life had been one of perpetually hiding what she was. And what of the Betas? Had they felt the pinch? Had they been tired of proletarian toil? Had they suffered oppression?

Alphas too had fallen victim. Claire's own father had lost all social standing with the suicide of his wife. Before the body was even cold in the ground, the government had ordered them to leave her childhood home and move to a neighborhood just above the Lower Reaches—Claire's father publically condemned as failure undeserving of midlevel life.

That new home had been damp and cramped. On the rare warm days, the air outside had stunk of garbage. Her father had weathered it with a smile and constant jokes. He had done everything for her, as if he'd suspected she was Omega long before puberty confirmed it—and was trying to atone.

Never once had he told her not to use the soaps that made his daughter smell like a Beta. He'd paid for her pills without asking her what they were for, made sure she had all the time she wanted with Nona.

Based on his personal experience, her father had known the world was unsafe for her, and he had done his best.

He'd known Thólos was miserable and bad, and shielded her from all of it long before Shepherd's targeted campaign had turned the city against itself.

Her mate said what no other Alpha would dare. He'd called the leadership deceivers, the citizens swallowing every word…

It made them worse still. Thólosens chose to bow and cede to his will out of fear, not because they took his words as gospel. It was because they were bad. Why else would they use the new paradigm to riot, rape, murder, indulging in the darkest parts of the human experience?

Shepherd had once said that it was not his Followers responsible for the violence. If Claire was willing to admit the truth, even she had never seen them do evil on the streets. No, their evil had been openly conducted at the Citadel. It had been her neighbors —like Mr. Nelson who she'd seen stealing from her apartment. It had been her mentors like Senator Kantor, in charge of the resistance but doing nothing.

It had been Premier Callas throwing women into the Undercroft.

Claire's free hand absently slipped to rest atop her belly, a poor shield over her son as if to protect him from her personal agenda, the wasteland, and her darker thoughts.

Everything was going to get worse.

"You're just one man." Troubled, Claire looked up and met Shepherd's eyes. "There are millions under the Dome. Desperate people transform. Soon they won't be afraid of your virus. It's only a matter of time before they come for you."

Shepherd took in her hand on their child, the blankness of her expression, and knew what she was thinking.

He scowled deeply.

Internally the Omega was a jangled mess, yet outside Claire remained placid, her face emotionless, and Shepherd greatly disliked it. He'd rather she cry and purge, than remain blank… reinforcing her misgivings. His mouthy, strong Omega was poisoning herself.

Shepherd called an end to their stroll. He swept her into his arms. She didn't complain, she didn't notice. Even marching her back into their room, where Claire was safe in a familiar place did not alter the flatness.

Food was brought; she didn't want to eat.

He purred; she stared into space.

Where was his thank you? Where was his reward? She should have been content, praising him… humming! Why was she being difficult again?

Instead, the Omega began pacing like she used to, fretting and wringing her hands. And then she did something that pushed him beyond the pale. Claire lay down on the floor, nonverbally refusing their bed, frowning as her eyes traced the cracks in the ceiling.

The seething mountain had had enough. Standing over her, Shepherd ordered, "If you wish for rest, you will rest in our nest." He then pulled off his shirt, holding it out so she might get up and place it accordingly, giving her one last chance to act on her own.

Claire waved a hand at him and made a snorting sound.

He nudged her with his toe, eyes narrowed, growl deep. "Get up."

Claire shook her head and spread out further on the floor.

He'd drag her to the nest if he had to, break her of such behavior. Leaning down, preparing to tug her up, Shepherd put his face in her line of sight. "Get. Up."

Claire planted her foot right on his chest and pressed him away, hissing, "Piss. Off."

The male froze, eyes flared in furious disbelief she'd had the audacity to physically challenge him, to look at him with such eyes... to hum out of tune on her end of their bond even though he'd given her what she wanted.

A meaty fist wrapped around her ankle. Claire showed her teeth, and that was all it took to push the monster to react. She yipped when he yanked her leg, the Alpha falling upon her so fucking fast the Omega never stood a chance of escape. Twisting until he contained her, he *toyed with his food.* Allowing Claire to wiggle and slip, Shepherd made a mockery of her strength, so that she might find how utterly useless such resistance was.

Claire wrestled with every ounce of old anger. Grunting and hissing, freeing an arm only to lose its mobility a second later, kicking a leg that was pinned in a heartbeat. Hardly aware, her nose went to his neck. Out of nowhere she groaned lowly, the strange burning thing inside her growing more satisfied by the struggle. When he moved again, when the rippling bunching flesh shifted, Claire got her arm free and instead of clawing her way out, she found her fingertips running from the hollow of Shepherd's throat down his defined torso, the Alpha arching immediately into her touch, his ribcage expanding in a great breath.

When Claire stretched just enough to mouth the mark she had made on his shoulder, Shepherd growled in absolutely violent bliss.

Nails raking harshly down the male's hard stomach, she made an impatient squeak, her voice thick with frustration, and the one thing he always craved from her, need.

"Shepherd." Arching up so her mouth rested against his ear, Claire's voice thick and filthy, animalistic and dark, growled in a maddeningly filthy lure, "Help me."

With a roar, one huge hand roughly rolled her under him face down upon the concrete, and yanked her body until her saturated sex was flush with the massive erection confined painfully in his pants.

Breathing hard under a vibrating mountain of muscle, Claire could hardly register the feeling of her skirt being tugged up, or the sound of a zipper breaking before a punishingly hard thrust filled her to the brim. Shepherd snaked his arm under her torso, gripped her by the front of the throat, and understanding dawned. His Omega felt weak from her loss of the war. She needed him to prove he was stronger—strong enough for both of them. That was their way... a relic from the Undercroft he'd taught her.

"Scream all you want. Fight me." Shepherd licked his lips and eyed her jerking body each time he forcefully fucked into her slippery pussy. "You won't win." A thumb swiped over her pulsing carotid artery. "You want to be conquered by your mate. Constrained submission calms you when you rage—when you feel lost and confused."

Compressed as she was, slippery and scented, Shepherd shoved in hard when she snarled, relishing the ooze of more Omega fluid and the wet music he created over the sounds of her purging anger. He began to describe the tight feeling of her cunt, how it was his to satisfy, how he would fill her and she would relish every last drop of his come, even if she fought—because he knew what she needed, and as her mate, he would give it to her.

The Alpha's voice was so saturated in guttural possessiveness, in greed, in the arrogant confidence that she was his to dominate; it sickeningly only made her want more. Each pounding thrust was angled to mercilessly bring friction at that raw craving inside her. The rapid smack of his balls against her, the slight burn from such a stretch, the intoxicating sounds of his loud, vicious grunts, and the almost too tight pressure of his fingers gripping her throat, fueled her urge to clench around him.

She shuddered, felt the walls of her cunt tighten like a fist, all the while ranting out a long list of venomous nastiness. Claire blamed him for her torment, for the deaths of her friends, for all the darkness in the world. It only made him more animal, dangerously savage as he constrained her and conquered, doing exactly what he threatened to do—jamming himself deeper, filling her to the point it scraped her warring emotions blank—transforming her insides to the point that Claire began sobbing out his name over and over, begging him to stop, begging him to fuck her harder, begging for something she could not name. Her pussy seized in an overburdened release. The knot was shoved deep, she screamed into the floor, and the male roared so loud at her ear it added an edge of fear to her bursting relief, extending Claire's frenzy and making her squeal.

It was not until his meaty hand on her throat loosened its grip that Claire began to feel the end of her wild, shattering climax. Soothing fluid was pumped so perfectly inside her, her body greedily taking it all while her Alpha whined low in his throat with each extended gush.

He was crushing her, her face mashed into the ground, his panting form seemingly content to continue to hold her trapped. Claire could not move, she could hardly breathe, yet his loud labored gasps were music, pressing calm to replace exercised rage.

She began to hum brokenly between pants. Shepherd stretched, rubbing his sweaty skin against her as he began to purr in praise to her perfect response to his domination.

Knowing to offer comfort after such a savage mating, his weight shifted so he might turn them side by side. Locked deep in his mate, knotted, and supporting the exhausted woman in his arms, Shepherd began to pleasure her gently with his hand—rubbing the labia stretched around his shaft, circling her clitoris, enjoying her twitching with each soft pluck.

Claire did not understand what he was doing, Shepherd never having fingered her in such a way when they were fused. Melting, still so sensitive, she tried to push his hand away, but he hushed her and continued to give soft pleasure that built up into an easy cresting wave of warmth. Still full of him, stretched and possessed by the knot, she gave herself over, drowning in what he offered.

He felt her internal reaction around his girth, the new pull that drank in the last drops of his lingering come, even though he could not climax with her. It was still very pleasing, each ripple and milking compression, the fact he had offered his mate the comfort she needed—something tender after so much necessary savagery.

All of it for her.

When he had drawn out every last ounce of her second orgasm, his hand left her pussy and began to trace the various angles of the exposed side of her face. Ghosting over her cheekbone, her lowered lashes, swirling around the shell of her ear, Shepherd asked, "Did I hurt you, little one?"

All Claire could offer in response was an exhausted, unintelligible whimper.

Shepherd pressed his lips right to her ear and purred richly. "Did I *please* you?"

A grunt, almost inaudible, came out on her breath.

Shepherd chuckled, relishing the pulse of his knot and the feel of her tight cunt still fluttering, her body speaking for her. "You pleased me, would-be Napoleon." He stroked her from shoulder to hip. "Your submission was beautiful."

Petulant, Claire reached down and smacked Shepherd's bent knee. "I am sure I will be feeling very beautiful later when I see all the bruises."

The nature of his growl lost all traces of tameness. "You chose the playing field. Had you not fought so savagely, I would not have restrained you while I claimed my prize."

She wanted to turn over, to look him in the eye, but the knot prevented more than a cursory glance over her shoulder. "Your prize?"

The male's deep chuckle shook her, Shepherd's fingers dipping into the top of her dress to pull at her nipples. "All of this is mine. You offered it to me when you began to stroke my body and placed your teeth on my mark. You promised it to me when you called out my name and begged. I gave you pleasure because I am yours. And feeling you come all over my cock, knowing your body takes satisfaction from mine, it is something I love to give you." Holding her a little tighter, Shepherd growled into the purr, lecherously fondling her breasts. "Confess that I fulfilled what you wanted. There will be no pouting or allegations."

Stroking upward, his big hand enclosed over her throat again, but did not squeeze, only encircled the smooth column, a possessive gesture that made her flutter down below.

Warm words were purred at her ear. "Confess, little one."

Disorder came from order, fear came from courage, weakness came from strength. –Sun Tzu

Disorder, fear, and weakness were all she'd seen wandering Thólos.

"You're my mate," Claire whispered. "You wanted instincts… and I'm all out of ideals."

He stroked her again, Shepherd's voice low and sincere. "I realize you are struggling to accept that everything was not as you originally believed. Growing wiser does not mean you failed. You should be proud that you possess the strength to face the truth."

It felt far more like losing her faith.

Shepherd caressed her body, teasing further arousal until the knot subsided enough that he could take her to the nest and begin again—eager for his reward and her attention.

Arms full of Omega, Shepherd lay back on the mattress, pulling Claire to straddle him. Voice velvet, he teased. "This time I will be your prize, and you can take me anyway you desire. I will even put up a fight if you want me to," a rich heady voice flowed, a smile thick in his voice. "And I'll let you win, little Napoleon."

Since they had opened the Premier's Sector, the rebellion's progress had been gaining almost alarming momentum. It had been too easy for the one now addressed as *Lady Kantor* to usurp Brigadier Dane. The resistance wanted a savior to make everything better after the Senator's death, and it looked as if one had appeared. None of the surviving Enforcers knew Leslie Kantor; she had no reputation, no fame or infamy. But she had a name—the same name as their newly dead hero.

All it took for the group to fall under her power was the name Kantor, her stunning smile, and promises of freedom from Shepherd's tyranny.

One by one, the resistance bowed willingly—all but Brigadier Dane, who seemed vastly unsettled by what she was witnessing.

It was not that Corday doubted Leslie; it was that he trusted Dane. Even if he didn't like his superior officer, after watching her tirelessly fight for the suffering people of their city, seen the look in her eye each time one of their family had been reported dead, he'd come to trust her instincts implicitly.

Brigadier Dane never openly spoke against Lady Kantor, not once she'd seen the Premier's Sector with her own eyes. She obeyed every order, but it was her lack of communication that Corday noticed most. He knew her well enough to see the older woman discerned what was important; she knew what was at stake, and she understood the importance of unity... and the danger of what even Corday could see was a developing demagogue.

People went missing under the Dome every day; it made Lady Kantor's ability to swell her hidden militia simpler as the weeks passed. A small portion of those missing people, those with no surviving family, who had lost everything—those hand selected by Leslie—joined the ranks of an organized and dedicated rebellion.

To join her cause, was to offer your life, literally.

Leslie Kantor spoke a great deal, her speeches fiery, the flagging men and women under their banner once again alive with faith. She said there was no need to fear infiltration again; they were untouchable now, simply because those recruited to join their crusade and enter the Premier's Sector were not permitted to leave until the day they would take back the city.

The only souls who could pass through that secret underground door, were those charged with maintaining a charade. Brigadier Dane, Corday, a few key members of the original resistance, were ordered away to continue their lives outside the rebellion's inner workings, to meet regularly, Leslie Kantor occasionally amongst them. In the same house where Senator Kantor had once laid out his plans, Brigadier Dane now laid out the sham of hers.

She had been ordered to serve as head of this puppet resistance, a great many of those who followed her having no idea a shadow organization had sprung up within their numbers.

Day in and day out, Corday did his duty, and day in and day out the *resistance* grew weaker while the rebellion grew stronger.

Unlike Brigadier Dane, Corday had been back inside the Premier's Sector more than once to confer with Lady Kantor. Each time he'd returned, those who had been chosen, seemed more like Followers and less like citizens. There was a fire in their eyes when they looked to their leader, a zealotry that made Corday nervous.

All in the name of progress...

Leslie had taken to the dead Premier's desk. His office had become hers, even though not all the bloodstains could be removed from the wallpaper or carpet. She always smiled when he entered; she always stood from her chair, circled the desk, and greeted him with a kiss on the cheek.

"I am so glad to see you, Corday. What news have you brought?"

"Fifteen of our men died last night trying to procure a shipment of food." He wasn't talking about the soldiers she had gathered around her. He was talking about the original supporters of the resistance who were still in the dark about what was going on here. "Shepherd's men defended their cache. Every case of fresh produce made it into the Citadel."

"They didn't die for nothing, dear Corday." Leslie put a hand to his cheek; she offered an expression of deep sadness. "They served as a distraction so my team might acquire a great deal of fertilizer left forgotten on the farm levels. Our first mission was successful. Those men and women's sacrifice will be remembered."

No one had discussed this with him. How could she knowingly have let him lead his men to their death? "A team left here on your orders?"

Smiling, Leslie nodded. "Yes, a small squad, hand-selected by me. I trust them implicitly; last night each one of them proved they were worthy of that faith. Soon, we will have everything we need to craft military-grade explosives."

There was one major impediment to Lady Kantor's grand scheme, one Corday could not be quiet about. "We still do not know the location of the virus."

"Your men have scoured the city with nothing to show for it for almost a year. Shepherd must keep it in the Citadel. We burn that building to ash, set off enough explosives to incinerate everything inside, the virus will be destroyed. Wasting time searching, as my uncle did, got us nowhere." She took his hand, squeezing his fingers as she led him to sit so she might serve him a drink. "The true rebellion is about action."

Watching her pour coffee from a china pot into a decorative cup, Corday wondered if she knew how ridiculous such an act of congenial etiquette was when they were talking of inciting a massacre.

If the plan was successful, several city structures would collapse, burn, bury people alive.

Tens of thousands could die. But, if Shepherd's regime fell, millions more would live.

Corday didn't want the coffee, he didn't want to sit in a lavish bloodstained room. He wanted his people to be free. "Claire is in the Citadel. You gave me your word that no attack would commence until she was rescued."

Nodding, Leslie considered, offering an alternative. "The classified data cubes housed here have blueprints of the Citadel, the underground, even the Undercroft. Take them, study them, chose the most likely locations she might be held. On the day of the attack, I'll send teams ahead of the blast. It will be a coordinated effort."

Spinning the golden ring on his finger, twisting it around and around, Corday turned his furious attention to facts. Should the plan succeed, when Claire learned what Corday had agreed to be a part of, she would never forgive him. But if it worked... she would be free. The survivors in the city would be free.

Whispering, aware what she offered was a monstrosity, the beauty urged, "Asking our men to divert their attention from freeing their families to rescue a woman many here see as a traitor would undermine our mission. This is the best I can offer you. Sacrifices must be made, Corday. I think even your Claire would understand that."

Taking her seat behind the desk, Lady Kantor became nothing but business. "Now, I will be honest with you. You may find things on this data cube you'd rather not know. Don't dig too deep. Keep to the maps."

Claire lay fast asleep when Jules' voice sounded beyond Shepherd's door. The Alpha had worn her out as he was wont to do. Knowing she was unconscious when he was called away was a small relief in the storming sea of Shepherd's growing agitation at the interruption.

Jules had not tried to contact him via COMscreen. There was only one reason the Beta would have dared approach and physically knock on the door: Svana.

Slipping silently from the room to see Jules waiting in the hall, Shepherd scowled. His second-in-command stood with many soldiers, ordering them to take up guard outside Shepherd's door as if war threatened from above.

There was also something very disturbing about the set of Jules mouth when he spoke. "Svana is on the premises. She waits to *parlay* with you."

The Beta's word choice was utterly unamusing. As if Claire might hear through the reinforced steel vault she was locked inside,

Shepherd spoke lowly in their shared language. "She has been off the grid, out of range of your trackers for weeks. Describe her approach, was it elusive? Apparent?"

"I have yet to decipher her point of origin, but I can tell you, she was first spotted in the GW94 tunnel walking from east quadrant. She wanted to be seen."

Considering how long she had been *punishing* them with her absence, Shepherd had some choice words to share with the Alpha female. "Did she bring the virus?"

Jules fell into step with his leader, blank and focused. "If it's on her person, it remains unseen."

Looking to the COMscreen offered by his second-in-command, Shepherd watched a feed of Svana fingering through schematics spread on the main table of the Followers' Command Center.

"It's unorthodox. Spying on your men will lead them to believe you don't trust them." Shepherd wanted to be angry. More so, he wanted to not feel relief his second had acted in such a subversive manner.

Jules didn't trust Svana and it was no secret. He was thoroughly unapologetic. "There is nothing in that room I have not anticipated she might see."

Shepherd grunted, the noise deep in his throat. It was neither an affirmation nor a negation.

The way the Alpha female had crept down there with no fanfare, spoke volumes. There was a reason Svana had breached the underground, and it wasn't to speak with him. She wanted something. "You will wait outside while I speak to her."

Jules turned down the corners of his mouth. "Understood, sir."

Shepherd was not finished. "But you will watch and listen through the COMscreen. I doubt she would suspect you would plant surveillance equipment in your own Command Center, especially since we know the resistance has partial access to our communications network."

"When I heard she was in our halls, surveillance equipment was not the only thing I planted in the room. I placed a micro-tracker on her person."

Shepherd had suspected what the Beta had done before Jules had confessed. "We will discuss what you've done later. For now, don't make me feel my faith in you has been misplaced."

Buried deep in his expression, was a small sliver of hurt. "Brother, I am loyal to you, always. Which is why I am telling you now, do not allow her to leave that room."

Shepherd made his final point before reaching for the door to his Command Center and leaving the Beta in the hall. "Svana killed Kantor. It's done and cannot be changed. So remember, without her compliance, we cannot subvert the population of Greth Dome. Without her, not one of your brothers will know freedom. You, we all, need her."

The hinges moved smoothly, even for a door of such size. As he had been ordered, Jules remained in the hall, cut off from his leader, glaring down at a dissatisfying exchange on his COMscreen.

Door sealed tightly behind him, Shepherd took a deep breath, and looked over his statuesque *beloved.* Glowing with health was such a cliché term, but it fit Svana well.

"Svana, you have been missed."

Her dark hair was loose, glossy, and clean. She pulled it over her shoulder as if to display its beauty, offering a soft smile. "I knew you'd be angry I was gone for so long."

Cocking a brow, Shepherd asked, "Was it your intention for me to worry?"

"No." She shook her head, contrite, her usual imperiousness waning. "Beloved, we quarreled. It was my fault. I know that now. Once I had some time to think, I realized a verbal apology would not be enough. So I have crafted something valuable to offer you."

Shepherd thought to lecture. "The murder of Senator Kantor was unwise."

Her laughter trilled, china blue eyes aglow. "On that point, I disagree with you. His death was necessary, though I won't pretend I didn't enjoy it."

There was no immediate rebuttal or argument, not from the Alpha male. Shepherd kept his silence until even Svana began to grow uncomfortable in the lengthening quiet. Not once did he move his eyes from her face, not once did he blink, he only waited for the inevitable.

When she began to look uneasy, he said, "Your actions prove redundant and provocative. You now owe Jules a debt you will never be able to repay him." Shepherd, fisted the collar of his coat. He measured his words. "We had already infiltrated the resistance. How does removing an advantageous pawn help our goal?"

"How does it not?" Svana walked closer, as if she expected to be praised. "His murder coupled with my manipulation of those fools, has caused our only opposition to disintegrate. As of now, they are powerless, scattered, and dying. I did that for you."

Shepherd crossed his great arms over his chest and scowled. "Svana, your role in our coup was to hold the virus and keep it safe.

Furthermore, endangering yourself in an attempt to dismantle an organization *I allowed* to exist is, in fact, subversive to our cause. The resistance offered a rabid population just enough hope to keep them lazy and waiting to be saved. If they have no souls fighting for them, they will begin to fight for themselves."

Svana was done playing, done trying to smooth over their dispute. Her voice grew hard. "They already have begun *to fight for themselves*. Your Omega stirred up the city with her flyer. Rebel recruitment increased, as did guerrilla attacks. Thousands of people keep her image in their pockets."

Cocking a single brow, Shepherd warned. "I caution you. Desperate Thólosens are nothing more than a pack of ravenous dogs. Remember, we are outnumbered and cannot leave until satellite imaging shows a storm free environment over the Drake Passage. Considering the season, our exodus could be months away. Do not stir up trouble."

Svana threw up her hands, half in defeat, half in exasperation. "I did not come here to argue with you. I came here to warn you." Reaching into her coat, the woman produced a packet of hand written notes. "You need to protect yourself."

Shepherd took the offered papers, and found the photograph of a man he despised. Shepherd hesitated, his eyes drawn to the circle of red marker around Corday's hand.

"Enforcer Corday wears a woman's gold band on his smallest finger." Svana's nonchalance slipped, her voice hinged on desperate. "Every time he hears the name Claire, or talks about her, he touches it, toys with it. When I asked him about the ring, he confessed. Has your Omega told you she's betrothed to him? Has she told you he promised her he'd end your life? Remember that while you are enraptured by your pair-bond, she has appointed another man to kill you."

Seeing her china blue eyes looking over him with pity and disappointment burned. Shepherd swallowed, squared his shoulders, pretended he did not feel a knife slice straight through his heart, and lied. "She told me. The confession was... cathartic."

"I see..." Svana braved placing a hand on Shepherd's chest, stroking up to touch the bare skin of his neck. "I am begging for you to forgive me, my love. Look through the information I have brought, do what you will with it. Please remember what we are to one another."

His voice, it came out worn and sad. "I never forgot, Svana."

"I know you are going to ask me where the virus is, and you expect I have been keeping it from you—that I will continue to keep it from you, as if we are in opposition and not partners looking to build a great future together." Heartache was open in her voice, in her expression, and falling in liquid testament from her eyes. "In order to reaffirm what we are, I've brought it. It's yours."

Reaching into the layers of her clothing, Svana produced a biohazard banded cylinder, the thing so small and unassuming, it was hard to believe what that little device was truly capable of. Inside something smaller than Svana's fist lurked a nightmare, the very disease that almost eradicated the entire human race.

She offered it freely, her one bargaining chip gone. "Take it, my love. I don't want you to have reason to doubt me."

The cylinder was placed in his hand. Closing his fist around it, Shepherd sighed. "When you act on your own without talking with me, I fear for you. It was not a question of doubt."

Voice dropping to a whisper, Svana's eyes shifted to the man's scarred lips. "I wish I could kiss you."

The tension softened in Shepherd's face; he smirked. "I will kiss you the day you take your throne and free our people."

"Yes, that will do." A warm smile on her mouth, Svana slipped away and eased towards the door. "Goodbye, Shepherd."

The virus now in his power, he let her go. "Goodbye, Svana."

It was three minutes before Jules dared enter. "She's gone, spotted above ground moving east."

Once the door was sealed, Shepherd looked to his second-in-command and saw that the Beta fully understood what had just happened. The Alpha cracked his neck, the man miserable under a stone-faced façade. "Have this analyzed to confirm the virus is inside and the containment untampered with."

Jules displayed the depth of his feelings in one infinitesimal hitch of his brow. "You lied to her."

Yes, Shepherd had lied to her, because Svana had lied to him first. "Have this room swept for surveillance equipment *you did not plant*. The guard stays outside my room, even when I am there."

"Yes, sir."

Chapter 4

While folding laundry, Claire sensed the link chime like soft bells. The sensation was a fair deal calmer than the inferno she'd felt over the last hour. Shepherd had been exceptionally angry, Claire was relieved he'd gone and that the rage was not directed towards her.

And then she'd worried something was terribly wrong. Misgivings came with the manipulation of the pair-bond. Worse was the doubt. Claire never did know just what stirred him up, and they both knew he'd remain mute to her questions. He never told her anything about how his time was spent tormenting Thólos... as if she'd forget what he was.

A warm hand slid down her flank. "You are thinking of me."

Claire jumped under the unexpected contact, yelping as her heart leapt into her throat. Since she'd bitten him, he had taken to sneaking up on her, lingering in the shadows... watching her. It was always unsettling, Claire unsure if he'd been doing so all along.

Now, the link was *open*—he could not hide from her.

"If your plan is to murder me by scaring me to death, you're on the right track!" Claire glared over her shoulder, barking, "I should sneak up on you and see how much you like it..."

His lips were against her crown, the beast all grumbly and soothing. "You would never be successful in such an endeavor."

One hand cupping the subtle bump of her belly, Shepherd enfolded her in his embrace, offering a treat on the palm of his other hand.

She snatched it at once, shoving a chocolate in her mouth, all the while arguing, "I might not be as sneaky as you, but I am a lot faster."

"Yes." Shepherd grew marginally annoyed at the reminder. "You are very fast. A good trait for an Omega. Gloating, however, is less desirable. Eat your chocolate."

And there was that other new thing, the smirk he was learning to inspire. Claire popped another truffle between her lips, slaked and impish. "So you are trying to feed me candy until I'm fat and slow?"

Shepherd purred, enticing the Omega when he rolled his groin against her. "My mate is a glutton, but I exercise her often."

Mouth full, Claire argued. "Sex is not exercise."

Shepherd nestled closer, thoroughly pleased she'd engaged in a playful back and forth, and very eager to reward her. Or he was, until Claire backed away, her scent suddenly laced with sharp anxiety.

Shepherd watched her fidget and dart her eyes to every corner, he watched her waver between anger and alarm.

Distraction typically realigned his mate, and he was perfectly comfortable with manipulation when the outcome would make her calm. Maintaining the distance she'd put between them, Shepherd cocked his head. "What have you painted today?"

Claire waved towards the table so that he might look for himself before she began to sniff at the air.

Keeping his eye on the woman, Shepherd approached her work. A cursory glance went over what was splashed on the paper. He saw her point of view of the very afternoon he'd first laid eyes on her. She'd painted him to be monstrously large, herself small, draped in rags, holding a bottle of pills. Jules stood sentry, his cool-eyed disdain captured perfectly. Every detail was beautifully done. He would have told her so, but in his heart, Shepherd knew his appreciation of that moment was not what she'd hoped to encourage.

His pleasure would inspire her pain. Claire only ever wanted him to see more and be moved to change. He already was more—a great deal more.

He waited for Claire to make her speech, to offer her insight and whatever lesson she'd cooked up all the hours he was away. Instead, she ignored him, nervously toying with the bedding.

Shepherd cleared his throat. She didn't look. He chose a neutral comment of their shared memory. "You pulled down your scarf to swallow one of those pills. You exhaled. That was the moment I first caught your scent."

Claire stilled. Her eyes didn't leave the nest, but she did speak. "How many hours did I stand there?"

"Six." Shepherd set aside Claire's painting, leaning a hip on the table. "You stood in the Citadel for approximately six hours."

A line formed between her brows. "It felt like much longer. I'd been so sick, but I could not leave... because you would not acknowledge me."

"Women come to the Citadel daily to offer themselves to me or my men. All are ignored."

"I'm not sure what to make of that statement..." The idea made her skin crawl. Claire worried her lip. "You could be wrong. They might only wish to speak with you."

Shepherd's offering was gentle, the man crossing the room so that while he spoke he might trace her claiming marks. "You were different, little one."

She didn't mean to cringe. Claire knew he had not intended to insult her, but she did feel something. It was not a good feeling. Truth was, Claire understood the motivation of such women.

After all, had she not done the same thing, trading her body to Shepherd? “Not in the long run.”

He absorbed her reaction, her poorly veiled shame, her misconception of injustice. Fingers burrowing into her hair, he purred all the louder. “You are my mate, Claire. Not a whore. You carry my child... There is no correlation to what those women offer and what you share with me.”

Claire looked back at the table, thinking to edge around him. “I can understand why they would offer themselves. I do not appreciate that you call them whores. They are just trying to survive.”

He could have made a snatch for her, he could have pinned his mate to the bed to show her his displeasure with her hesitation to be near him, but Shepherd let her be. It was more than her abnormal scent, she was acting very strangely.

Again he gave her space when she walked away.

When she got to the table, out of nowhere she set her fist to the wood and snapped at him, “Why did you not bring a tray?”

Because he had spent the last hour in conference with Jules, furious to find that Svana had indeed stripped off every stitch of clothing she’d worn underground and stashed them in an abandoned home. “Your meal is being prepared as we speak.”

"Oh..." Recognizing her rudeness, the blush in Claire's cheeks, the tone of her voice, was self-conscious. The flush deepened an instant later, embarrassment replaced with growing agitation.

She circled back to the bed, brushing past Shepherd and began to sniff the air again. Turning on him, eyes narrowed, the hiss came back to her voice. "Something is wrong with this room. Did you change something while I was sleeping? Move something?" Her attention darted all over, Claire growing breathless. "Fix whatever you did."

Shepherd narrowed his eyes, unamused with the strangeness of her behavior. "I have changed nothing."

"No. no." She looked at him, had the nerve to point and blame. "Something is different; something is not right in here."

"There has been no alteration, little one."

She growled and fisted her hands. Right before it seemed she might start shouting, she seemed to snap out of it. Confused, Claire forced a softer tone, stammering, "Of course not... Everything looks the same."

"Is there something that you desire for the room?" Shepherd cocked his head, measuring her every breath. "Something you think is missing from our nest?"

"No." She tugged her hair, once again looking around and very uncomfortable. "Yes."

"You are behaving as if your nest were threatened." As if that explained everything, the man crossed his arms over his chest and waited for her to confirm that he was correct.

The weight of the glare she leveled at him was monumental. Rationality fled and Claire shrieked, "It is, you jackass. The room is wrong. FIX IT!"

"In what way?"

Was the man an idiot? Beyond caring, she threw up her arms. "I DON'T KNOW! If I knew what you had done to the room, I would fix it myself."

"Do you want me to leave?" This was not normal; Shepherd needed her normal. "To retrieve your meal at once?"

"Yes." She spun around, changing her mind, "No. You have to stay. This is your fault. You don't get to leave until you fix whatever you did."

Shepherd stood taller, commanding, "On the bookshelf, top far right, is a book with a white cover. Bring it to me."

Claire huffed, shuffling her bare feet over to what he demanded. She grabbed the only white book and threw it right at the man. It bounced off his chest, landing on the concrete with a thud.

The Alpha growled—it was not the guttural call to mate, it was a warning, a threat, and something that would have sent grown men white as a sheet. Claire ignored it, choosing instead to wring her hands and pace.

He came upon her so quickly that when a great arm slipped around her middle and hoisted her up, she shrieked in surprise. Once seated at his desk, Shepherd pulled her to his lap, held the squirming Omega still, and opened the book. The giant flipped through the pages, stopping when he found a marker, and raised the book to the female's eye level. "This is what our baby looks like in his current week of development."

Claire stiffened, staring at the glossy page.

He tapped an underlined paragraph. "And here it says that at this stage in pregnancy, hormone fluctuations will occasionally make you exhibit irrational behaviors." The arm about her middle tightened, the greatly irritated male growling, "Take note, little one, that I am being extremely indulgent of you at this moment."

She felt his nose at the back of her head, heard his deep intake of breath, and read the book's offered list of tips for the father. He was right, she was acting crazy. Nodding, she admitted, "I think you may have followed 'how to handle pregnancy mood swings' to the letter: 'Do not argue, offer food...'"

A small gleam in his eye, Shepherd agreed. "I did."

She was a little embarrassed. "Considering your temper, I suppose I should be impressed."

With the mood seeming to have passed, Shepherd sought out the trigger. "Articulate what brought on your distress."

"I have no idea."

The Alpha had the audacity to chuckle, the skin at the corner of his eyes creasing.

Still annoyed, Claire muttered, "You're a bastard."

He gave her hip a light smack. "Watch your mouth."

She began to protest, wanting up. "But the room is wrong, I can feel it. And I *need* more chocolate, and I hate the grey walls, and I have this weird urge to eat charcoal, and you stink of Svana." Her mouth snapped shut, green eyes beginning to burn once she recognized the truth in her words. He did reek of Svana! Growling like she might rip out his throat, a haze of fury clouded her every thought. "**That is what is wrong with the room**!"

Dashing the book against the wall, Claire inhaled deeply, her nose to his chest.

Wisely, Shepherd held still, let her crawl over him so she might find the limits of where the scent might linger. He'd caused this discord by unthinkingly not considering such an outcome, but he would not allow Claire to believe the worst. She smelled him everywhere, clawed her small hands into his clothes, finding every last trace. The stink was so subtle, she was surprised she'd even noticed. The man did not smell of sex or slick or a recent shower. In fact, he mostly smelled of her.

Cautiously, Shepherd offered a remedy to the issue. "Shall we bathe?"

We?...

Claire pulled away as far as his hold on her would allow. She repeated what he'd crowed only moments before, the phrase much more menacing coming from her lips. "Take note, I am being *extremely indulgent* of you at this moment."

Shepherd drew breath as if to speak, but Claire held up a finger, and cut him off. "You stink of the Alpha you fucked in my nest a minute after you found her trying to murder me and your baby! Speak and I might just have to kill you."

The Alpha kept his mouth shut—but it was not her tone or threat that stopped his lips, it was the smell of his mate's arousal already seeping, hot and thick, into the fabric of his trousers. He watched her small hand hike up her skirt, saw her reach under to cup her sex. Once her fingers were covered in slick, she met his eyes, smearing her hand down his neck, directly over the spot where he stank of his *beloved.*

Gathering more of her wetness, Claire soaked the patch of his shirt until she could only smell herself.

It was not good enough.

Unable to comprehend anything beyond black rage, Claire clawed the fabric and ripped Shepherd's shirt to threads.

Her nose went back to his exposed chest and she let out the most threatening growl an Omega could make.

If he was hushing her, or reprimanding, touching, or in shock, Claire was absolutely oblivious. Every fiber of her being demanded she stake claim, that she scratch her marks all over his body, that she leave a sign all other females would see.

She left him bloody.

Breathing hard, she reared up until eye level with the man. "Now you will fuck me, hard, in every way that pleases me. And when it is done, you will get me food, because I'm fucking hungry!"

He was on her with such force the breath was knocked from her body. Shepherd did exactly as his mate demanded, pounding into her with a fury that set her howling amidst their shredded clothing. In Shepherd's experience, there had never been a coupling like it. She was beyond estrous, beyond fiery passion. Her angry possessiveness blended so beautifully with the lustful need to claim what was hers—but it was so much more than that. What began as violent evolved until they were more than physically joined. He had what he wanted, her covetous emotion honest and pure in the bond. Shepherd gluttonously reveled in it.

She wanted *him*.

They had never openly discussed it, or even furtively shared whispers after the sham meetings they pantomimed week after week for Shepherd's surveillance team. Both Brigadier Dane and Enforcer Corday had played their parts, openly quarreling at the old location, hosting meetings where nothing of value was accomplished. It was all a performance, but the continuous suffering of their people was very real.

The old resistance was dying. Their friends were dying—not just from violence, but from crushed hope. In the eyes of the Dome, Brigadier Dane and Enforcer Corday were two great failures.

The title did not disturb either of them. Both clung to what really mattered: survival.

Not their survival, both of them could see the writing on the wall. They needed their people to live; they needed to give Leslie Kantor and her growing band of rebels a chance.

At least that's what they told themselves.

More people died, more disappeared.

Since the day Lady Kantor told him in secret exactly how she was going to take back the Dome, Corday could do nothing but nod dumbly. It sat there, that horrible knowledge, like a rock on his chest, but he could not see any other options.

Brigadier Dane had needed to know what her actions would be consigning, what the two of them were a part of.

That's why they found their way to one another the first time they'd met in secret, how they found their way to the ruined safe house where the headless remains of Senator Kantor still lay wrapped in garbage bags on the table.

The causeways were empty, the city hollow, and cold, the two standing in a room that reeked of decay.

There was no one there to watch. Lady Kantor and her minions, Shepherd and his Followers... no soul knew who met and why.

No one ever visited the corpse. It was more than the smell; after all, the entirety of the Dome stank of unburied dead. People didn't come here because only three people knew whose body was decomposing in that room.

They stood with the table between them, eyeing one another with open animosity and desperation.

Lady Kantor, her misused leadership; what it was costing those who'd valiantly served, had grown out of hand. Too many people were dying, 'necessary sacrifices' she would say, so her growing band of handpicked revolutionaries might build bombs from garbage. Bombs they planned to strap to their bodies on the day the *chosen* would free the city.

As usual, Brigadier Dane's voice was filled with disdain when she addressed the younger man. "You have never been a good Enforcer, and that is because you questioned everything. Insubordination, anything but blind obedience, was not allowed to flourish under this Dome. The wise ambitious do as they are told until they reach a position where they give the orders. Then there is no need to question, because everyone else must obey. It seems you've finally learned this lesson."

And that right there was the reason it had been so easy for Shepherd to seize the city, and so easy for Lady Kantor to wrestle control of the resistance into her hands with only the Kantor name to validate her. "And what part of yourself was sacrificed to attain the rank of Brigadier?"

Brigadier Dane did something unimaginable—she lifted an eyebrow and actually smirked. It was such an unusual expression to see on the hard woman's face, that it was vulgar. "I have seen enough of the workings of this city. I have done what I could, knowing more could only be accomplished if I rose higher. Sacrifices? You become numb to them. You hang on to an ideal, and you strive not to forget it."

The sickness that had brewed in Corday's belly for weeks, churned. "If you are trying to justify the things we saw on Callas's Data cube—"

"Me?" the smirk became a sneer, Brigadier Dane cutting off Corday's quick-tempered complaint. "Boy, what you have done, your imprudence... can you even begin to grasp the consequences?"

There was a reason they came to this place, where the pair of failures might whisper in the dark, because there was no safe place to question amidst the fanatics rising to Lady Kantor's secret cause. Corday was not afraid of Brigadier Dane's disapproval, or in admitting he'd made a grave mistake. "Leslie Kantor..."

"Men like you are so easy to influence— you know everything, feel too greatly without questioning *yourself.* She pegged you for what you were the moment she took that first whiff. As Brigadier, I've seen veiled ruthlessness, the rise and fall of those who would attain the title of Senator. She is nothing new, a politician through and through, who hid in a room for the first months of this occupation thinking only of herself. When she was forced to leave or starve, she ran straight to her powerful uncle, saw an opportunity, and is using us all to achieve the highest goal a person like her might attain. The amount of people who will die when those bombs go off, the chance we might bring down the Dome, she is willing to risk all that and more to become the new Premier."

"The enemy is Shepherd."

The woman let out an extremely agitated breath. "How blind you are. The enemy has never been Shepherd. The enemy is us. We are fighting ourselves!"

"What you are saying is treason."

Brigadier Dane didn't give a fuck. "There is no government left to judge me. All that is left is Leslie Kantor, her ambition, and those so desperate for reprieve they will believe anything she proclaims as if the Goddess herself speaks."

The words passed almost tonelessly, from Corday's mouth. "If I move against this mission, I won't stand a chance of saving Claire."

"If you believe Leslie Kantor gives a single fuck about your Claire, then you're even stupider than I thought." Brigadier Dane ran her hand through her short, clipped hair, shaking her head at the man's foolishness. "Have you never noticed how often she mentions your Claire? Why do you suppose she does that? Does she mention her often in front of her *rebels*? Do they hate her?"

Corday shook his head, unsure how to answer.

"The Omega is lost, we all know it. The only thing Claire exists as now is the strings Leslie pulls to make you dance as her puppet."

The temptation to strike what had once been his commanding officer, was so strong, Corday forced himself to take a step back. “I don’t trust Leslie Kantor’s motivation any more than you do, but she has lit the spark Senator Kantor failed to ignite. She might be our only chance.”

“Yes,” Brigadier Dane nodded. “She has set the wheels in motion and there is no stopping them now. But two people can *question*, they can alter the future if both of them are ready to pay the price.”

“I promised Claire,” Corday hissed, disgusted and tired. “I have maps of the Citadel. Leslie gave them to me.”

“Leslie Kantor did not give you the Premier’s data cube so you could save Claire. She gave it to you so you would grow to hate the man whose corpse lies between us... She gave it to you so you would grow to love her in his place.”

Leslie had warned him not to look into the files, and of course it was the first thing Corday had done. Every Senator had a secret, some of them monstrous.

“What he did to Rebecca...” Leslie’s ploy had worked. Once Corday had read the file, seen horrific video footage, he had begun to despise the old man. “His dead wife was the reason Senator Kantor would not let us enter the Premier’s Sector. Knowledge of his crime would have been uncovered, he would have been exposed.”

"Boy, Premier Callas had something on everyone, and everyone had something to hide. But when Rebecca died, I saw the change in Kantor myself." The hard woman looked down at the wrapped corpse; she frowned. "For the first time in his life, when he spoke of *the people* under the Dome, when he spoke of bettering ourselves, he meant it."

"I cannot forgive him for what he did to that poor woman, her husband, and their children. The footage of those boys' murder burns me every time I close my eyes."

"Leslie was shrewd in her dissection of your," Brigadier Dane smirked again, "ethics."

Grinding his teeth, caught in the riptide of all the bullshit around them, Corday hissed, "How else do we stop Shepherd?"

"We don't."

"What?" His patience, his understanding of the woman before him, was worn out.

"You've left us with no options. Lady Kantor's attack on the Citadel will take place. You will be at her side as it burns."

Corday knew what she was driving at. "You want me to kill her..."

"After the bombs go off, right as the citizens rally." Brigadier Dane, nodded.

"I'll be busy searching for Claire!"

"No, you won't. The only member of *our* resistance who can truly search for the Omega is myself. If this is what it takes, I will give you my word I will find her or die in the flames trying. So accept the fact that Leslie is not going to spare you, a known figurehead of the old rebellion, when she might have you at her side to inspire our troops to follow her into war. You have value, and unlike me, she trusts you. You'll be in position. One bullet to the head will take only seconds, then you can kill Shepherd, or you can waste your life searching for Claire while the Citadel crumbles around you."

Absolutely not. "I would be killed the second I pulled the trigger. You are asking me to risk my life, to fail my friend? For what?"

"Don't tell me you don't see it. I know you do. There is something wrong with that woman; there would have to be for her to do what she did to her uncle."

"No..." Corday had never fathomed that Leslie might have done such a thing. "She didn't."

Crossing strong arms over her chest, Brigadier Dane asked, "Since when has Shepherd not advertised his exploits? When he infected our brothers and sisters in Judicial Sector, their deaths were broadcast over every working COMscreen under the Dome. When he hung the Senators, it was done before jeering crowds. Why make a secret of Senator Kantor's demise? Why take the head off the pike?"

It was too convenient to be conceivable. “One woman would not have been able to accomplish all that was done in that night. The body parts, the missing Omegas, it isn’t possible!”

Dane nodded. “And doesn’t that frighten you all the more?”

Chapter 5

Conceal your dispositions, and your condition will remain secret, which leads to victory; show your dispositions, and your condition will become patent, which leads to defeat. –Sun Tzu

Well, she had failed that one. Miserably...

Claire had no idea what had come over her, but the sign of her lapse into madness was a visual Shepherd took much pleasure in displaying. His chest and back were covered in lines of scratches artfully done; her own little pattern that made it clear they were not marks gained in a fight, but adornment of a sort. More so, they were mesmerizing and she had trouble keeping her eyes from them every time he entered the room and removed his shirt for her nest.

And he was doing it on purpose.

Shepherd wanted to show them to her, he wore them proudly. Hell, she would not be surprised if he had made a point of displaying them to his entire army. A situation that was infinitely humiliating for her, was nothing but delightful for him.

Whether it was the pregnancy or the pair-bond, Claire didn't know; all she knew was that she had not been in her right mind. Maybe the book had been right. She'd been absolutely irrational and could not stop the furious blush that came to her cheeks every time she found him looking at her with those eyes.

It was that same damn expression he'd favored her with after she had painted his portrait.

Catching his eye again, glancing away as she felt the color rise to her face, Claire heard the memory of her voice demanding that he fuck her, explaining in filthy detail the exact position she desired, how fast he was to move…

Shepherd enjoyed calling her coy in the past, and gods if she didn't feel that way now.

There was no scolding on his end for her demure behavior in the aftermath, or how she tried to keep her distance and her eyes to herself since. Shepherd was simply patient, sitting with her as she ate, offering her a piece of chocolate every time he'd seen her since—as she'd belligerently vocalized a *need* for it.

When he did reach for her, a thing that was as inevitable as breathing, there were ages of purrs and long caresses until she was sedate and melting, even smiling softly as she arched and hummed. It was in those moments she would distantly recognize her fingers were tracing the marks she'd placed on his body, having memorized them; enjoying the feel of the slightly raised wounds.

He had just taken her again, employing the exact same position she had twisted him into that day, only having moved far more luxuriously so that she might feel it all with her legs folded between their shoulders, bent in half so that he could plunge in as deep as possible. When it was finished and she was tame, Claire lay on his chest, green eyes following the path of her hand as she asked, “How many weeks have I been back?”

A rumble deep in the sedated Alpha’s rib cage answered, “You have been back home with me for eight weeks.”

Home?

“This is not a home, Shepherd.” There was no rancor in her voice, just soft words as she stilled her fingers and woke a little from the stupor. “It’s a bunker underground in a city full of evil.”

A palm came to her cheek, pulling her attention from his flesh to see the hungry smile in his eyes. “That is correct, little one. Thólos is evil.”

The warmth of the cord deflated and her voice fell flat, “We both know it’s not that simple.”

He answered her with a long slow stroke down her naked spine. “That is not the reply you would have made six months ago.”

“Six months ago many good women I knew still lived; the city was not totally in shambles.” Her calm began to evaporate and sadness took its place. “Six months ago I had not met you.”

“And you were starving to death... hunted and tormented by your fellow citizens.”

"And blissfully ignorant of just how ugly the world could be." Claire sighed, feeling his thumb pass softly over her cheek.

"Look at me, little one," Shepherd ordered in a soft voice. When her gaze came back to his, her expression just a little challenging, he promised, "All that was done here, it will only inspire a better world."

Fanning her hair over his chest, Claire pressed her ear to Shepherd's heart. Tracing the muscles over his ribs, she sighed. "The very idea what you have done, what the people of Thólos have done, might improve the world, makes it a world I don't want to live in."

He hushed her and played with her hair, knowing that she meant every word. A moment later Shepherd's great body shifted, pouring her off of him so that he might ease down above the pouting Omega. Pressing his scarred lips to where his son grew stronger daily, Shepherd inhaled. One large hand came to feel her there, to seek out signs of new life in the subtle swell of her skin.

Eyes almost dangerous, Shepherd spoke in a voice one uses on children, explaining to his baby, "Your mother is speaking nonsense." The expression he leveled at her even as he traced patterns on her belly would wither grown men. "She thinks I do not know what is in her thoughts—that I have not recognized her avoidance of any mention of you, my son." The palm of his hand closed over her little belly and he gripped it as if to reassure the life inside. "But I know she would never follow through on her plan. Claire O'Donnell would never harm her child nor would she suicide and abandon you like her mother abandoned her."

The blood drained from her face, her heart seemed to drop out of her chest, and Claire gaped. He had exposed her; he had upended her lie.

Rearing up, looming his bulging mass over her, Shepherd held her guilty stare and stated harshly, "Because you love him." Unsure if he moved out of compassion or if he was trying to draw out some type of confession, Shepherd moved back to where he had been and gathered her up so that she might rest on his chest again in her preferred position. "You would never hurt your son."

It was an underhanded tactic, but underhanded was Shepherd's specialty. The male was making a point he knew she had yet to address: Thólos, or her baby. It was a complicated position for Claire that only led to denial of the issue. Taking her survival day by day, pretending there was no child, was all she could do without going mad.

Thólos had to be free.

And then what?

Shepherd's reign might fall and she would be without the Alpha who fathered the small thing inside her. Corday's resistance might fail, and the remainder of her days would be spent underground in a life unworthy of her child while Thólos still suffered.

Either way, she could not endure.

A corner of her mind spoke over the mental chatter, whispering incessantly that her baby could never stay there—that Thólos was not good enough, and it scratched and scratched, infesting, and reminding her that she had a duty to her unborn son, that he was more important than any other life.

It was getting harder to silence that voice every day.

So in war, the way is to avoid what is strong, and strike at what is weak. –Sun Tzu

That is exactly what he was doing to her, even if he was holding her comfortably as he jammed in the knife.

Talk of the baby was acutely painful.

As if he knew, warm, reassuring arms wound around her, Shepherd held her with love and murmured that she need not fret, that she need only remain patient.

What she needed was so far beyond patience. She needed to strike back.

"You are the strongest Alpha I have ever seen," Claire began, compelled to make her point. "You have limitless potential. But, just like this unborn child, you are trapped in the dark. The acts of bad men shaped and distracted you. Serving your mission, even after you climbed from the Undercroft, you were never given a chance to be part of the world, Shepherd. Like me, you have never been free." Her eyes went to where his hand had frozen in a caress over the life they had created. "So what of him? Will he live a mimic of your life? Will he wield murder and pain against those he's taught to hate?"

Shepherd began a slow languid stroke that ended at the scruff of her neck. Gripping Claire's nape as if she were a kitten, he held her immobile. "You do not know of what you speak, and that is no fault of your own. So listen when I tell you that our son will be raised to greatness... nurtured and educated. Loved." His voice dropped, grew chilling, and he growled, "But far more importantly, how could you imagine I would inflict upon my child what was done to me?"

Face impassive, Claire spread her hands on his chest. She had one weapon, the truth. "Svana was in your company days ago. What have the two of you planned for this baby? Will your schemes, your examples, make him the next Premier Callas?"

It was like watching a storm gather in his eyes. The silver went dark, the rage began to build, and the man's expression grew almost violent. She wanted a strong response, and she got one... she got even more than she anticipated. At last, she had struck him where he was weak. It was not her accusations that had burned him, it was that forbidden name: Premier Callas.

Leaning on the link, she felt Shepherd's boiling animosity. But there was more, Shepherd was seething with disgust.

Widening her eyes, she grasped the secret; Claire knew exactly what inspired the hostile feelings buzzing on Shepherd's end of their bond. There was only one reason to harbor such hatred. She knew it because Shepherd had given her cause to feel the same way.

Claire said it again, just to be sure. "Premier Callas."

The Alpha's end of the link turned rancid, old anger crashing down between them like a wave of acid.

It was more than what that monster had done to his mother, it was jealousy.

Jealousy...

Claire could hardly believe it, couldn't even begin to fathom why, but she knew—It was Premier Callas, Shepherd's enemy, who Svana had been unfaithful with. It had to be for him to feel such betrayal.

Looking away from the feral mate who was silently raging, Claire fell into her thoughts, shaking her head like it could not be true. Premier Callas was responsible for the torment and death of Shepherd's mother... why would Svana harm her lover in that way? Resting her head on Shepherd's chest, she stared at nothing, shared in his pain through the link, and felt as if the floor had fallen from under them both.

Like thoughts of the child growing in her belly, Claire had pushed memories of the exotic beauty away each time they'd cropped up. It had felt essential to maintain her sanity and her composure when faced with the man who had defiled their bond by fucking the Alpha female. But she had to look, had to face the discomfort and sadness that squirmed in her insides when homicidal china blue eyes flashed to the forefront of her mind.

She had to, or she would turn into Shepherd—a man who had buried such anger as if it might just disappear. The link was slowly assuring that such a demise would be inevitable... his personality was just too strong.

Svana's was a face Claire could never forget. That beautiful, frightful image carved into her.

It was as if someone had shattered a window, light pierced the darkness in her mind. The wide eyes and soft lips... she'd seen them before. Claire had never paid much attention to high society or politics. Of course she, like everyone under the Dome, recognized the key players: Premier Callas, Senator Kantor...

But Claire had seen her somewhere before.

The woman had been dressed differently underground, less glamor, less makeup, but still radiant—incredibly beautiful.

The magazine...

Claire had had it on her coffee table for months. The woman on the cover of *The Thólosite* was dressed in a gown and smiling like the princess of the city. Claire had bought it for an article on cooking, but the woman on the cover had also inspired the purchase, Claire thinking the softly waved hairstyle was something she might try herself.

What was her name? Why was Claire suddenly sick to her stomach?

It had been printed in big block letters.

There was a soft intake of breath when Claire came to terms with her blindness. How could she have not recognized such a thing when the knowledge might have been useful to Corday?

Her voice shook, her veins turning to ice. "Her name is Leslie Kantor..."

"You will not think of her, Claire."

"She was important enough to be on the cover of the *The Thólosite.* I cut my hair to look like hers... I am a little copy of your beloved, just like she said."

Shepherd narrowed his eyes. "You are nothing like Svana."

A rough snap came from Shepherd's end of the thread, as if the male demanded she stop the direction of her thoughts. Claire ignored it and opened her mind to stutter though everything that flooded in.

Leslie Kantor, Svana, had been underground only a few days ago. She had touched Shepherd, communicated with Shepherd... and she was out there, in Thólos working to destroy the city. That was why, that horrible day months ago, the woman implied she saw Shepherd rarely.

Muttering under her breath, impatient and equally horrified, Claire said, "Kantor is a very powerful name."

Shepherd removed his hand from her nape, laying his arms stiffly at his sides, where the mountain's fists clenched until his knuckles became white. Idly hushing him, petting his flank, Claire hummed, deep in thought, her actions merely instinctive as she stroked the angry Alpha sweetly. Shutting her eyes, turning her face to nestle in the musculature of his chest, she shut everything but what she saw in her mate. Her mind fought to piece it together, feeling as if she was on a precipice, that the moment held a great value that she needed, that Thólos needed, that Shepherd needed.

She felt physically ill, plagued by all the anger bearing down on her from the male. The link was aflame, her eyes pricking. When she could bear no more, Claire leaned up, her humming ended, and she put her fingers to

Shepherd's chin. His face was turned away, the man pointedly looking elsewhere. Silver eyes were boring a hole into the wall instead, and even Shepherd's scent was full of the warning musk of imminent violence. So Claire sat up and began to sing to him, a soft song in a pre-Dome language she suspected he would find pleasure in.

The fire of his eyes jerked in his skull and settled on the little thing straddling his chest. He growled at her, not sexually, but with immense threat. Her voice did not waver, the song continued, and with strength of purpose she lured him. The beast continued to watch, to follow the movement of her mouth, and Claire saw his neck twitch, saw him swallow and fractionally relax.

The last refrain passed her lips, the music ended, and she did not start again.

With a voice grainy and dark, Shepherd demanded lowly, "Do you know the meaning of those words?"

"I have a general idea."

"You sang that you loved me, that I was the one you longed for—that you would grow old in my arms."

"It was just a song, Shepherd, sung for a man who was angry and needed to take a breath."

Bitter eyes watched so very carefully. "And so you are offering your mate comfort."

Claire had touched him, she had petted him, she had done it all for that very reason. "You once told me that bruised emotions would not serve me. They will not serve you either."

One hand unfisted, meaty fingers reaching up to twist around a strand of midnight hair hanging over her breast. "You are far too clever, little one."

Not clever enough to have failed to notice something so important sooner. "I want to know about Svana."

"And you wish to offer some trade with me for knowledge?" he growled derisively, angry, because he could see plainly what his mate thought to bargain with.

"You could just tell me," Claire added, absolutely serious.

"I could." A malicious light turned his expression to evil, the pad of his thumb ghosting over her lips. "But I won't."

He was expecting her to deny him, pushing her so she would drop the subject and he could win with minimal effort. But she couldn't. The very fact he was reluctant to discuss what he sensed in her thoughts made it clear it was something she needed to know.

Her purpose had not been forgotten.

Thinking back on the conversation with Maryanne, the idea of redemption, Claire frowned and asked him softly, "Could Shepherd change?"

"No, little one. In this I could not."

And it was so heartbreakingly sad. Feeling her eyes well, looking into the face of her captor and her Alpha, Claire met mercurial eyes harboring an expression caught between insult and reassurance.

She drew a deep breath and offered the only thing she had left. “If you answer all my questions, I will give you your kiss.”

Voice cold as death, Shepherd spoke. “It is not so simple, Claire. If you wish to speak of our history, to know of my Followers’ inner workings, then you must prove you are dedicated to me in every way. I will need much more than a kiss.”

But she had nothing else to give him.

Shepherd stated plainly, “You will tell me every detail of this plot you’ve thought to carry out against me.”

She shook her head, scowling slightly. “What plot? You know what I want.”

“You are lying, little one. You think you have been cunning in the war you wage. But I have decades of experience and have outmaneuvered your every move. There will be no negotiation. Either you give me what I want, or I tell you nothing.”

Claire did not even hesitate to lay out exactly what she desired. “I want you to fail in Thólos, Shepherd. That is not a secret. Even pair bonded to you, even carrying your child, I would stand against you in this matter for as long as I could. I also won’t pretend I don’t partially understand your motivation, that what I saw out there didn’t sicken me. But a cause that uses the suffering of many, innocent or not, to make your point, is something I could never condone. I have to believe in redemption or all I have done has been for nothing."

"I already told you the resistance was fully infiltrated months ago," Shepherd explained, his voice was riddled with disgust. "You were not duly upset. The reason you accepted my words was because you hope, you believe your Corday might overcome the invisible prison he's trapped within."

"My Corday?" The pit of her stomach dropped out, Claire understanding just who Corday had been smiling at out of frame of the pictures Maryanne had brought her: Svana. "Are the pair of you really so insidious?"

"The reason I was called away before our first dinner together, was because Senator Kantor had been beheaded. Since that day, the resistance has crumbled into dust."

Claire blinked twice, her face impassive, and felt that flicker of guilt knowing the resistance had been infiltrated because of her, because Corday had been seen with her. Green eyes looked to his chest, to where they were chained forever, and she tried to convince herself that Shepherd was lying, that he was trying to trick her.

He was not.

She'd been the one lying... lying to herself. And she could have stopped all of this if she'd only ignored her pain and focused on fact. If only she had let herself recognize the woman sooner and warned her friends.

Shepherd always flipped the table on her in these battles, outfoxed her with cutting information he could wield like a weapon. Not today. Today she would make her stand and she would not back down.

Claire shared her story. "I was warned by Senator Kantor himself, that should the city be made aware of who I was and what I was to you, that the resistance would hand me over. I was told I had to be hidden. I begged him to reconsider, argued that his best chance would be to use me and the baby as a hostage—inciting a rebellion at once in hopes you would not unleash the virus. He declined. In that moment, I knew any operation that mirrored yours, that counted one life as insignificant, would fail. The truth is, I have had no faith in the resistance. My faith is in the few unruined by you. My faith is in the few who survived your worst and came out better."

He took her jaw, held it gently but strong enough to make a point. "Do you really think you're going to win?"

Her repulsion was obvious. "We both know that I am not going to win."

"Did you give him your ring?"

Black lashes lowered and a pair of tears ran over pale cheeks. “It was my mother’s. He found it in my house while I was trapped here. Corday returned it to me after I jumped off the roof. The morning I decided to kill myself, I slid it on his finger, so he would have something to remember me by.”

“Did you ask him to kill me?”

“No.”

Shepherd’s chest expanded in a great breath, as if relief might have found a way inside a heart so black.

Claire chose to correct his moment of emotional reprieve. “I did not ask him to kill you, I didn’t encourage it. His oath was offered without my prompting.”

Shepherd looked at her as if she were the most deceitful thing he had ever beheld. “Do you love him?”

Her hand came to where Shepherd cupped her face, her move on the game board not yet finished. He had made specific demands, and she would see them through, she would show him that she was stronger. Turning her face into his palm, into the heat of a hand that had crushed throats, beaten the weak, that knew every curve of her body, she held his eyes, her own laced with worry for them both, and pressed her lips to his palm and kissed. “I have given you what you demanded.”

"Not everything," Shepherd answered, absolutely unashamed. A large thumb traced the lips that had just kissed his palm. "Love me."

That worming thread was so needy, so invasive and searing, and his wants were so remarkably simple, animalistic even, but she could not give in to him. Claire swallowed, and leaned into his hand.

Shepherd spoke first, as if he knew the very Sun Tzu quote and intention she had in her mind, "It is easy to love your friend, but sometimes the hardest lesson to learn is to love your enemy."

Seeing her eyes widen, hearing her soft inhale, Shepherd explained, "I watched you read The Art of War at the Omegas' hiding place. You have used its lessons well, little Napoleon." He pulled her closer, drew her near until their lips brushed. "The night you marked me, when you touched me, I did feel your affection. Other times as well. I know you care for me. I also know that you don't want to, just as you don't want to care for the baby you adore who grows in your womb."

Claire was walking thin ice and she knew it. "The night I marked you I pretended you were the husband I had waited for, the one who loved only me as I loved him... that there was no sticky evil permeating our link. No ruination. No disappointment. No Svana I had to share you with," those words had cost her and it was written all over her face. Claire pressed, saying that hated name again, "Svana, the woman who pretends to be Leslie Kantor. She is the one who overtook the resistance."

Shepherd nodded, his eyes taking in every facet of her expression, tracing parts of it with his fingertips.

Steeling herself, drawing in a breath to face a greater opponent, Claire fought the demands of the link and outlined the little she knew. "Before the breach, it was Leslie Kantor who set this nightmare in motion. You told me she came to the Undercroft, discovered you. She whispered in your ear, in Senator Kantor's ear... in Premier Callas's ear." His hand on her cheek slipped down to her shoulder, gripping her claiming marks as Claire added, "And because I can feel how strongly you loved her, I believe that you were unaware of Svana's intentions towards your enemy. You did not know of her affair with the Premier, not at first."

Shepherd did not nod or agree, he remained silent which was answer enough.

Claire took a breath, and spoke what the link whispered to her, "She seduced him, you destroyed him, and your Followers took over Thólos. But there is something very important that you have failed to mention during our talks in the past. I suspect the reason, the real reason that motivated this madness, has been hidden from me."

The Alpha was stiff, his eyes smoldering as he corrected, “I was honest with you in regards to our purpose. Thólos must be cleansed of evil. It is why the Followers exist.”

“Your beloved, she laid with the man you hate most,” Claire put her fingers over Shepherd’s heart, “and put grave pain here, pain worse than any torment you’d survived in the Undercroft. And still you follow her.”

“Claire...”

Looking him directly in the eye, Claire risked pushing him past the point of no return. “We are too different in our ideals for love to ever be easy—especially given... what happened, what still happens.” Her voice caught, unsure if it was his suffering or hers that threatened to drown her. She took a moment, and then gave the last fraction of herself. “And that gives me pain, because I would like the dream, more than you could ever know. Affection is natural, I see that now. But love...” she shook her head, “If I was to allow myself to love you the way things are now, it would destroy me.”

“You will kiss me again.” He demanded, something strange in the recesses of his gaze.

“For the rest of the night if you wish,” Claire countered, unwilling to bend until he broke. “But the cost was the truth. You have not given me that. Tell me, admit to me what she did.”

Breath labored, Shepherd continued toying with a strand of her hair as if it might bring him comfort. "Svana fornicated with Premier Callas to create a child that might carry the Callas bloodline's superior immunities. It was her belief that future generations would be enriched, that the resource, no matter the man, should not have been wasted."

"That is a lie—one you don't believe anymore than I do." She leaned over him, looked him dead in the eye. "The probability of an Alpha female conceiving with an Alpha male is slim to none—even with the help of pharmaceuticals. She is not pregnant. If she wanted his baby, a woman as calculating as Svana, the woman responsible for the fall of our government, would have covered all bases—had him use a condom so she could collect his semen and tried in-vitro—kept him alive and imprisoned, where she could harvest what she needed from him, like you did to me." Claire sat straighter, glaring at the male who was linked to her forever, feeling her anger and personal outrage mingle and surpass his. "That's not why she slept with him, Shepherd. Svana did it because she is a sick emotional predator, shameless and self-absorbed; because her agenda is flawed; because she..." her voice faded away and she stopped herself before she went too far.

Vehement, Shepherd bellowed, "Say it!"

Deep panting breaths stretched the Alpha's ribcage. Claire knew when she spoke he would strike her, but it was another brick she could take from his delusion, a price she would pay. This was the very reason she waged the war.

Looking into his eyes, her own soft with pity, Claire cupped the cheek and spoke with certainty. "Because Svana never loved you. She never could have to have done such a thing."

The blow never came, instead something strange happened. Shepherd's eyes welled, and the monster Claire could hardly think of as a man did something utterly human. He spilled a tear.

It was only one silent drop of salt water, yet it must have cost him greatly. Claire brushed it away in the kiss he wanted, soothing him as he had done for her each time he'd brought her to tears—only she did something he never did, she felt remorse at another's suffering and offered with trembling lips, "I am so sorry, Shepherd."

Her words made the man screw his eyes shut. When Claire tried to shift, to move away and leave him in peace, his arms snapped around her, squeezing, holding as if she might vanish to a place he might never reach her.

Claire settled closer and asked softly, "Would you like me to sing you another song?"

He nodded once.

Chapter 6

When her song had finished, Shepherd held her where he could look at her, the man staring for hours. It made her uncomfortable, the intensity of his scrutiny, but each time she turned her head away he would gently bring it back so that the green of her eyes was not denied to him.

Their cards were on the table. Claire had proclaimed Svana did not love him, and in doing so proclaimed he was a self-deluded pawn. The revelation cutting him deeply, though she suspected it was something he already knew and laboriously struggled to accept. Shepherd had accused her of harboring thoughts of killing their child before Svana or Shepherd might ruin him. She did, and it made her hate herself for all the doubt that flourished inside her, how every day her resolve weakened.

Neither was at peace, each of them raw from battle. But Shepherd was still bigger and he would not let her move.

Between them the thread was... a nameless sort of discord. And it kept changing, evolving. A part of Claire wanted to continue the assault, to demand that Shepherd stop this madness in Thólos now that he must accept Svana for what she was. The wiser part kept her silent.

When you surround an army, leave an outlet free. Do not press a desperate foe too hard. –Sun Tzu

Confronting him about Svana, it may have been Claire's greatest victory against Shepherd yet, but she took no joy in the deep-set anguish she sensed in the Alpha. Nor did she feel content in the confessions she'd made to get what she wanted. She may have brought him to his knees for a moment, she may have bluntly torn at his delusion, but for some reason, she wondered if she had not given him, an unscrupulous man, more reason to fight.

Thólos was a plaything for Svana, an entertainment and ploy for some endgame Claire could not grasp. Thólos was a mission to Shepherd, a man who had been a lifelong inmate in one sense or another—a man who truly believed in the cause. Following through on the mission, Shepherd wanted to do it to save them all; to even save Claire from herself.

Maybe that's why Shepherd was looking at her; maybe he was afraid for her. Or maybe he had finally seen the purity he seemed to adore was gone. Perhaps now that he knew everything, now that he realized the truth, he would kill her. A part of her wanted him to. Watching his eyes, the unending stare, the hardness and calculation, Claire felt her bottom lip tremble just enough to give her wretchedness away.

Flexing her muscles, sick of his game, Claire found again he would not allow her to retreat. Just like with each other time she fussed, Shepherd's answer was to place the weight of his palm on her chest and increase the incessant purr only long enough for her to still again. All the while those eyes were moderately narrowed, heavy upon her, communicating something she could not even begin to fathom.

It seemed like hours passed before the mass of the Alpha finally lifted and set her free. At once, she left the nest, locked herself in the bathroom, and tried to find solace in the solitude. There was no comfort there, not in the haunted face of the green-eyed woman staring back at her from the mirror.

She bathed and attended to the needs of her body, stretching out the time, hoping that when she left the steam filled room, Shepherd would be gone.

Claire was not so lucky.

He was there waiting for her, still naked, standing proudly near the nest.

Stern, his brows drawn low into a scowl, a large hand came forward. He flicked his fingers, still silent after so many hours, and beckoned her forward.

Claire shook her head in the negative, feeling exposed and awkward. The man did not hesitate to approach, to take her by the shoulders, but it was not with a harsh, punishing grip. Shepherd was holding softly, rubbing her chilled skin with his thumbs.

When he leaned over, when their faces were only an inch apart, Shepherd let one hand slide down her arm to take her fingers in his and bring them up to touch his face, placing her palm over his scar spattered stubble.

Shepherd was calling forth the debt.

The timing could not have been worse. Claire did not want to kiss him; she didn't want to touch him. All she wanted was to hide from those eyes and burrow in her nest. Her cowardice made her feel weak, and she was tired of feeling weak. That was why she forced herself to draw his head down the final distance so she could touch her mouth to his and be done with it.

The sensation was strange. Shepherd's plump lips were not foreign to her, he'd pressed them uninvited to hers many times, but something about applying pressure back... about actually kissing him... it made the experience completely different.

The slow extended moment of a simple kiss, Claire still heartsick over their conversation, knowing he was too, the almost cautious fusing of their lips felt... it made her feel a little better.

In the past, living as a Beta, there had always been an issue of growing aroused. Slick was an aroma no soap or pill could cover. That was the reason she'd never really kissed a boy, not even after the end of a date. Just a quick peck if anything... similar to the platonic way she kissed Maryanne. Yet standing with him at that moment, hardly moving, hardly touching, Shepherd's kiss was utterly different. It was decadent and soft, the feather light slide of his mouth on hers pleasurable.

And he seemed so patient.

Claire suspected that he was giving her time to feel it out, as if he knew she was a novice. When it seemed the natural time to stop, she let her heels hit the floor, and looked at his mouth, rubbing her lips together as she wondered if it had been done right.

"Yes." Shepherd said it softly.

Claire hardly had time to address the fact that he had answered her thoughts before a low rumbling throat noise came from the Alpha. He backed her against the wall, and with a breathy groan, retook her mouth.

Shepherd feasted, grunting the second she hesitated—a damn bully, until she followed his lead and ended up breathless and dizzy.

Where there had been silence, an aggressive purr filled the air. Where there had been discomfiture, there was loss of sadness. Claire had never known kissing could be so consuming, so fulfilling, that the act could be so very intimate.

Between the assertive purr, the strength of his hands roving all over her body, and the long forbidden enjoyment of his mouth and tongue, Claire felt the transformation from ragged to something reconciled. Everything was different, but it wasn't, but it was. Every breath in her lungs came from him, air they shared, and when he made the growl, it was not because he needed to call forth the slick, for she was pooling with it. It was simply because he was an Alpha calling to his Omega mate.

Reaching down he hooked her legs over his arms, lifted her against the wall. He opened her up, without ever breaking the contact of their mouths. The first spearing thrust of possession was almost enough to draw out her climax. Claire felt him smile against her lips, and whined when he pressed biting kisses down her jaw, her mouth tingling and hungry for more attention.

Brimming with Shepherd heavy and thick inside her, the Alpha tasting every inch he could reach, Claire found herself mirroring his movement. She kissed his neck, bit his ear as he often had done to her, lapping at the shell. When her actions brought the man to slam his fist against the wall, it didn't frighten her. Deep, under layers of complications, worry faded, because she felt safe. Fear disappeared, because she felt loved. And the link sang that so long as she remained in that room, so long as she was bound to the Alpha adoring her with his mouth and body, she could be both those things.

Her arms were wrapped tightly around his neck, the Omega climbing a thrusting mountain, until she claimed his lips again. He seemed almost surprised, the flash of silver between his lashes only thrilling to her. The rut turned far more aggressive, a part of Claire wondering if he even realized how desperately he moaned as he jerked against her body.

She could almost hear his thoughts: *Take your victory...*

That's what this was. She'd made him vulnerable, she had the power, and that was why he had stared... gauging if she knew. It was rare for him to be the one to lose control, yet there he was, mumbling something against her skin, something soft and breathy, a sound very much like, "love me," over and over.

And god help her, she wanted to.

Shepherd's hips rocked, angled so he could hit that fleshy spot inside her, groaning when Claire keened appreciatively from his effort.

"Love me," he said it again, demanding and loud, absolutely unashamed.

The sensitive flesh of her swelling breast was fondled, a nipple toyed with as he surged. He smelled so perfect, tasted even better, Claire's tongue dancing with his, relishing Shepherd, mimicking the penetration of his cock. The feeling of him smiling against her mouth again was all it took in the end, a taste of his joy so much more exquisite than any sexual gratification. The swell of pleasure crested, broke through her as she held him tighter, Shepherd's name passing from her lips.

The saturation of the groan he made once the rippling strangle on his cock began, it wrecked her. She shivered, feeling him grind deeply to knot. They were both panting when their mouths broke apart, each gazing at the other, expressions opposite of the distrust and suspicion from before.

Watching his kiss-swollen lips form his declaration, "I love you, little one," was captivating.

Glancing from his mouth to his liquid silver eyes, Claire gave him the only olive branch she could. She took a deep breath, and claimed, "Your son is making me hungry."

Shepherd laughed, the rich sound that came out was beautiful when suspicion did not alter the tone. For just a moment, she was struck by the splendor of his smile. He kissed her long and deep. "Then I shall feed you. I will care for my mate and our child."

"I want raspberries."

The nature of his arms around her grew gentle. "I always make sure there are raspberries on the premises for you."

"I know you do."

Walking through the door with a scowl and bruised jaw was not exactly the picture Corday wanted to present to Leslie Kantor. She did not respond with favor to perceived weakness, and he needed her to keep him in her counsel. Brigadier Dane had been right. Leslie's talk of saving Claire had diminished. But, there had been a spark in her the second Corday handed over his analyzed maps of the Citadel, his notes, and tested her. "You might be right. Claire may have betrayed us. If your rebels can find her, there should be a trial."

He did this because he loved Claire. He did it because he knew Brigadier Dane was the only soldier who might actually care if the Omega lived.

Leslie's subtle hints had done their work. Around the Premier's Sector, the name Claire O'Donnell had become a whispered curse. He'd seen their contempt when the few rebels chosen for the rescue mission absorbed their orders. He felt it every time Leslie spoke of Shepherd's mate.

Day by day, he trusted Lady Kantor less. Day by day, he silently prayed for Claire.

Today, his prayers were answered. The morning had started simply enough. Scrounging for supplies was second nature at this point. Corday knew what to watch for, who not to look in the eye while he scuttled through the causeways.

Armed with Callas's data cubes, the rebels now knew exactly how to craft explosives, where certain chemicals were stored, and likely locations of other supplies the rebellion's growing numbers might use.

Once Leslie's list of necessities had been acquired, Corday began the journey back to the Premier's Sector, aware he was a target the second his hands were full of anything that could be deemed useful to another.

When the thugs came, Corday simply offered the box of random items to the three unwashed men, unable to reach his gun with his hands full. Before his supplies had even hit the ground, a boney fist connected with his jaw. He'd hit the snow, somewhat surprised a man so skinny packed such a punch. Another got him with a cheap shot to the kidney just as Corday saw the third pull a knife.

A shot was fired… but not from Corday's gun.

A woman old enough to be his grandmother stood on a stoop with a haggard face, aimed, and fired again. Two of the thugs had been hit—one dead, the other howling from a bullet to the leg. Asshole number three grabbed Corday's box and ran off, abandoning his bleeding cohort to whatever fate awaited him.

The woman shot one final time, the bleeding man took one to the chest, and she lowered her weapon.

Visibly shaken, far more frightened than he was, the lady offered, "Why don't you step inside for a minute. I'll make you a cup of tea."

She'd just saved his life. It was the best damn tea he'd ever drunk.

He learned her name was Margery, that all her family had died or gone missing as the occupation continued. She and several of her friends had taken refuge together in that apartment—safety in numbers—until those numbers started diminishing too. Being over sixty and a single woman in Thólos was a death sentence... she'd begun to despair, until she found faith in herself.

The woman reached into a pocket of her coat and pulled out something Corday had seen before, something almost everyone in the city still whispered about: Claire's flyer.

"If she can stand up, so can I." The way her gnarled fingers brushed the photo spoke of reverence. It spoke of pity and compassion—something Corday had not seen amongst the mustering rebel forces. No, they were hard; they had to be to have chosen to make themselves living weapons to serve the *greater good*.

Looking at Claire's picture was like a knife in the heart. Brown eyes shining with pain, he glanced away from the paper. "Claire was my friend."

"She's my friend too." Margery said, that same trembling hand reaching forward to pat Corday's hand. "Though I have never met her."

It seemed Claire had gotten her last wish; some part of Thólos had become inspired. And because of it, one old woman had just saved his life.

Claire O'Donnell was right.

Corday sat there like a dunce, worrying the ring on his finger as he talked about his time with the missing Omega. He let Margery fuss over him until the adrenaline wore off and her hands stopped shaking. He told her everything he could remember about his friend.

His supplies were gone, hers were meager, yet she packed him a bag of food anyway.

"There are more of us, you know," Margery offered, "passing around the flyer. We help each other." She gave him a fresh copy of Claire's picture, held out the food, as if she could draw him to the cause." Rheumy eyes shone bright as she smiled. "We have to help each other."

Reluctantly, he took her scant offering, certain it would do harm to the woman's morale if he did not let her do her part.

He was hours late by the time he returned to base, hours Corday had spent regathering the supplies Leslie Kantor needed, but he was not going to skulk in.

"Leslie," Corday called to the woman walking down the polished marble lobby of the Premier's mansion.

Her head was bent over a COMscreen, the Alpha female busy passing a litany of orders to the men following at her heels. Hearing someone use her name, glancing up to see one of the few who would presume to address Lady Kantor familiarly, she smiled.

Stopping in her tracks, she asked those circling to give her a minute. "Dear Corday, I have been worried."

China blue eyes got one glimpse of his face and she reached out cold fingers to trace the growing bruise. Despite the others nearby, Leslie took his hand, led him to a place where they both might sit. "What happened?"

"I was jumped by some thugs. They are all dead."

Her agitation was replaced with an expression of approval. "Well done. And to cheer you up, let me share fresh news of your Claire."

That was the last thing Corday had anticipated to hear. He forgot the pain in his jaw, far too focused on listening to anything relevant Leslie might know.

"The maps you analyzed, I have looked them over, as have the team chosen to free her. Based on food delivery locations, we don't believe she is in the Citadel proper," Leslie brought forward her COMscreen, pointing to a far corner of a schematic, "but here."

The place she pointed to was the top floor accommodations of a neighboring structure suspected to serve as barracks and training rooms to several of Shepherd's newer recruits.

"The food Shepherd has delivered here is of a finer quality than the rations sent to his Followers." The brunette was beautiful, she was charming, and she smiled at him as if the world were wonderful only because he existed. "Women's clothing was also seen being delivered. There is a room near the top, a window overlooking the land outside the Dome. This is where he keeps her."

Shepherd kept her underground, in his den where none could see her, not in some lavish apartment with sunshine and views. Claire had told Corday those facts herself. Leslie was wrong, or lying. That didn't stop him from vocally taking her side. "I knew you'd find her."

"In five days, you'll have your Omega back."

There was something in between her wonderful news that sent a chill down Corday's spine. He said what he knew Leslie wanted to hear. "If she is not in the Citadel, then in five days, I won't be breaking my oath to her. She can be collected later. The freedom of our people is paramount. Your uncle tasked me with your protection. Only you can save us. I choose to follow you into battle."

Lady Kantor threw her arms around Corday, hugging him hard. It all felt so staged, nothing like the warmth that he'd found in Claire's embrace.

It felt as cold as the air outside the Dome.

Five days were left before Shepherd would face the fire. The Citadel would be burned to ash, a great many citizens' lives lost while they huddled in homes crushed by falling debris. Buildings would collapse, panic would ensue. The survivors would have to take responsibility for rebuilding their future together or they would freeze and starve.

The woman standing elegantly before him, the way she spoke of sacrifice, saw in herself only a hero. The surviving masses would cheer her, a savior who led them out of the dark. Little would they understand, Leslie's plan may very well doom the Dome. The culpability was his, as were the lies, the desperation.

Enforcer Samuel Corday would be remembered as a monster, and he knew it. He was going to assassinate the woman he smiled at; he was going to allow her to carry out her plan.

There were no other options.

Lady Kantor's rebels remained on a tight schedule, the last bombs being assembled that very morning. In forty-eight hours they would be strapped to the bodies of twelve of the *chosen*, and then an attack organized to exacting detail would be unleashed in the midst of the afternoon—right when the Citadel was most crowded, when the causeways were full, when the highest probability of casualties would be likely.

Shepherd was going to die in those first fiery seconds, a great deal of his men were going to die.

Anyone within the blast radius was going to die.

There were not enough medics under the Dome to save even a portion of the civilians who would be wounded. And while their people suffered, armed rebels would be climbing over their charred bodies, bringing war upon all Followers yet unclaimed by the flames.

When their embrace ended, Corday took Lady Kantor's hand, made a point of doing so before the rebels gathered in the halls. He smiled his lopsided grin and thanked her. "To your victory."

Leslie placed her other hand atop his, wrapping his fingers in her hold. "To *our* victory, dear friend."

"For a man who is supposed to be some kind of scary soldier, you certainly fidget a lot when posing," Claire complained, dipping the brush in blue.

"I have better things to do, Miss O'Donnell, than stand around so that I can amuse you."

She could not stop her snicker at Jules's petulance. He hated every moment of her painting him, yet submitted to having her do it when asked... which meant the Beta had his own agenda. Looking up from the half-finished work, Claire looked to those unfeeling, but vibrantly colored, blue eyes.

Lifeless was easy to paint.

She translated what she saw, the scruffy quality of the man, the air of danger. "Are you going to tell me why you are allowing this? Or am I supposed to guess?"

The man had always been painfully blunt with her. "I wanted to observe the change in you."

"And measure it?" Claire asked, cocking a brow just to be bitchy. "Do you find me lacking?"

"I always do."

She chuckled again, peeking up to meet his eye. "I take that as a compliment."

The Beta stood a distance away, at attention, stiff yet twitchy... and glaring at her in that way he did. "You need to progress more. You need to accept what's in front of you."

The painting's final touches were rendered, Claire squinting at her project, looking for flaws.

"If I was to tell you how much I hate your enigmatic bullshit, would you believe me?"

"Thólos, Miss O'Donnell." The man grunted. "You can't save Thólos."

"I don't want to save Thólos." Setting the brush aside, she gave him a long look. "I want Thólos to save itself."

"And there is that clever brain I keep hearing about," the man snorted, rolling his eyes.

"For my only friend down in this prison, you're kind of an ass."

"I am not your friend."

"Yes, you are." She turned the painting towards him and watched his eyes flick down momentarily to appraise it. "I doubt you intended to be, but you are."

Jules always sounded so unamused, leveling that dead-eyed gaze at her. "You made me look different."

At his words, Claire burst out laughing.

Pushing the painting towards him, she mused, "I wonder if all of you see yourselves in some distorted way. This is what you look like, Jules."

Pinching the parchment between his fingers as if he found it distasteful, Jules lifted the painting and frowned at it. "I want to see your other work."

"Even the paintings of Shepherd?"

“There are more than one?” It almost seemed as if he cocked a brow, but there was no movement on his face.

For some reason the question embarrassed her and color flamed in her cheeks. Claire didn’t answer. She reached for her stack of paintings and leafed through them, removing several and setting them aside before placing the bunch before the Beta.

Unsmiling, he set his wet portrait down and began working through her collection, her images of Thólos, the nightmares she’d seen all there for him to examine as he flipped through the pages. Some paintings she could see were meaningless, boring to him. Some he stared at a little longer. There was no comment made until he reached the picture of Corday making eggs in his kitchen. “You should not have painted his rival.”

“Corday is not Shepherd’s rival. Corday is my friend.”

Flatly, Jules claimed, “Not anymore. Svana has him now. She’s turned him against you.” Those demonic blue eyes gauged her reaction. “It wasn’t hard.”

Of course she had. Leslie Kantor would have locked right on to him.

“You already knew...” For just a flicker of a second, Jules appeared intrigued.

Claire still had something to hold on to—something important the Follower discounted. In every photo she had seen, Corday still wore her ring. Whatever Jules, Svana, or Shepherd believed was not the total truth. So long as Corday wore that ring, he still had faith in their shared belief.

That was all that mattered...

A curve came to the corner of the man's mouth. "Do you still think I am your friend?"

Face bloodless, Claire looked up from where her eyes had been boring a hole in the table. Leaning back in her chair, crossing her arms over her chest, Claire countered, "And the Omegas? How have they been corrupted?"

"Do not worry on their account." He set down her paintings. "They are still cossetted and well-fed."

"And Maryanne?"

The jerk took a grape from the lunch tray Claire had yet to touch, popping it in his mouth. "Will get herself killed eventually. Nothing anyone can do about that."

Claire growled, menacing and angry. "If you eat one more grape off that tray, I will stab you in the eye with this paintbrush."

Jules actually laughed, every aspect of his face coming alive. But the burst was hoarse and almost unnatural, a long unused reaction that ended almost before it began. But a smirk remained. "During training I have seen the scratches and the claiming mark on Shepherd. You are quite a possessive little Omega."

"Be careful about who you call little, Beta."

Whatever false playfulness he had been enacting faded, but he was not offended, not even in the slightest. Putting his hands on the table Jules leaned over and asked, "When she tries to kill you, what are you going to do?"

The answer was simple. "I'm going to die."

The way his thin lips stiffened, Claire could see he was disappointed in her answer. "Your dramatics do not impress me."

"I think you comprehend a lot more about what's going on than even your leader. Shepherd knows she does not love him, she has used him, yet still he, like you, believes in something incomprehensible and obeys." Claire tapped her finger on the table. "With all this knowledge you both follow the psychopath we know wishes Shepherd's mate and his unborn child dead. The situation as it is, with men like you, how long do you really think I will survive? You and all your unsolicited guidance, friend, do not impress me."

Jules straightened and snorted. "You know what I see when I look at your pictures? All of them are finished. All but one." he tugged out the smirking self-portrait she had made for Shepherd weeks ago. "Tell me, Miss O'Donnell, why the portrait of yourself is only an outline?"

"Why don't you tell me, Jules." Her voice was as unfriendly as her expression.

"I once thought it was cowardice that held you back." The man shook his head. "I was incorrect. You are no coward. And yes, you are clever... just as clever as you are stupid."

Claire quirked her lips, fighting a smile at his lecture.

Jules ignored her and continued. "But I know what it is. I see you now." The painting of her was pulled from the others and turned so that it faced the artist. "You're willfully incomplete."

"It sounds like I fit perfectly into Shepherd's army of psychos."

"You lack unbiased perspective and throw so much motivation at the wrong problem... and you know it. Had you met Shepherd under different circumstances, this painting would have color. You are very lucky Shepherd fights for what he wants."

Gritting her teeth she snarled, "I fight. I fight every goddamn day."

The man shook his head of unkempt hair. "Not for him."

Looking away, sullen she grunted, "I fight for Thólos."

"Stop fighting for Thólos. Fight for your family."

With narrowed eyes, Claire leaned forward in her chair to confront the standing male. "And just who would I be fighting against? To me it looks as if the enemy is the same."

Jules put his hands on the table and leaned down menacingly. "You cannot have both and you know it. Thólos or your son—a city full of murderers and rapists, of people who have turned their backs on you—or your own innocent flesh and blood."

Frowning, ready to throw the barb back in Jules's face, Claire asked, "What would Rebecca have done? Would she have sacrificed her ideals?"

"In every way. My Rebecca willingly gave herself to Senator Kantor to save the lives of our children." The man spoke as if it was nothing, taking on his mask of lifelessness. "Yet he mounted her and made her watch as his soldiers executed our boys the very moment he made the claiming marks. He wanted a *free* Omega."

There were very few things in life that cut as deep as what Claire had just heard. It trumped everything she had seen in Thólos and pained her greatly. Slack-jawed, it took her a minute to speak. "I am sorry."

A flash of something dark came to Jules's expression. "No you're not. If you were sorry, you would want to make certain such a thing never happened again, no matter the cost."

Claire echoed his words. "No matter the cost."

And then he knew. "You still think your death would make any difference? You would throw away your life for nothing, destroy the child growing in your womb for nothing. Do you understand me? It would change *nothing*. Remove those thoughts from your mind."

Spine ramrod, Claire made no reply.

Cocking his head, Jules came to a decision. "Shepherd needs to be told that you are struggling in this manner."

"There is no need," Claire offered, her own voice laced with weariness. "Shepherd is standing right behind you."

Jules was still. There was no look of disbelief on his face or even a trace of fear, simply placid acceptance. At the first obvious sound of another man's breathing, the Beta turned and nodded at his leader. "Sir."

Looking at Claire, the Alpha barked at his subordinate, "You're dismissed." Jules moved at once towards the door. Once the sound of the locks was thrown, Shepherd took the seat across from her. "You know his name and history... he has freely told you these things." Shepherd seemed amazed and equally unsettled.

"You should not be angry with him. He is your greatest advocate, and I was the one who initiated all conversation." Urging him to not react negatively to what she'd revealed, Claire admitted, "There were times I needed someone to talk to, and he only did it for you. I know he doesn't like me."

There was a look in Shepherd's eye, buried under heaps of disapproval was a large dose of envy. "He has spoken on your behalf more than once. Jules *likes* you a great deal." Something was going on inside the Alpha, a stiff calculation of odds. "Do you always argue with him?"

"Always." She fought back the tick at the corner of her lips. "Your friend greatly enjoys reprimanding me."

Hooking a finger on the tray, Shepherd pulled it before his mate and gestured for her to eat. "You are behaving as if you feel playful, but you are upset. I am willing to discuss Svana and Corday."

"I don't doubt that for an instant." She knew he was trying to maneuver, and offered him a sullen smirk at his attempt. Claire picked at the fresh fruit. "I, however, do not want to hear you gloat about how my friend has been manipulated by your beloved."

"Little one." Shepherd leaned back in his chair and leveled her with those eyes. "You need not be threatened by her. I love only you."

After swallowing a bite of melon, Claire put down the fork. She let out a sigh, her expression falling flat. "If I say please, can we drop the topic? You have taken my world from me. I don't need to hear about how I have lost him too."

The purr began the second it was clear she was upset. "You have Maryanne."

"But for how much longer?" It was a pointed question that matched the sinking feeling in her stomach. "I feel like everything is slipping through my fingers and I don't know why."

"We will lay down now." Shepherd purred louder, standing and moving towards her. "Come, little one."

Frustrated, she complained at his course, feeling he did not understand what she was saying. "No amount of fucking is going to make me feel better about what I just heard."

He was already pulling her dress over her head, kneading the tension in her shoulders. "Time will soothe you and so will I. This is just one bad day. It will pass."

Chapter 7

"We are running out of time. Decide. Where is Shepherd keeping Claire?"

They were back in Senator Kantor's tomb, arguing over his body as they always did. "I DON'T KNOW where she is, Dane. That's the point. All I know is that she is in the Citadel."

Brigadier Dane, leaned closer to their shared COMscreen. "Show me a projection of the building's layout again."

"Claire jumped off the roof near the back." Corday explained, squinting at the image. "He keeps her locked out of sight, and would not have taken her far from his den, especially knowing her penchant for escape. She has to be near this location."

The older woman nodded in agreement. "And there are no windows in her cell; she told you it was grey, so no decorations either, only concrete. There must be running water for her use." Pointing to a segment embossed in the middle of the building's foundation, Brigadier Dane said. "She is here, somewhere on one of these two underground levels. Or she's here," Another branch of the building in a completely different quadrant was highlighted, "tucked between the loading docks and the ventilation systems. Both locations are fortified, few entrances. Once I am inside there will be even fewer exits."

Brown eyes hard with intention, he warned, "Bombs will be going off above you. The only plausible way to get her clear of the blast is to go underground."

"The Undercroft?" Brigadier Dane hummed, scowling over her thoughts. "There must be tunnels spanning the building, the very tunnels Shepherd used the day of the breech. Show me the maps of the prison. We need to estimate which locations he would have found strategic for invasion."

"These are outdated, originals from when the Undercroft was built. Shepherd's Followers may have designed a whole network of shafts not on these maps. If you get lost..."

"I don't get lost." Irritated, Dane's eyes flashed away from the screen. "So tell me, Enforcer, which one of these locations am I going to infiltrate?"

Sighing, knowing if he picked the wrong place to look for Claire, that she, that Brigadier Dane, would die, Corday said, "We need a second team."

"That is not possible." Dane had explained this before. "You know that is not possible. Not with two days. Not without Leslie learning what we plan to do. You have to choose one of these potential locations. You have to commit."

How on earth was he to do that without more definitive information? What if she was in neither spot? What then?

Brigadier Dane had seen him question himself over Claire's position time and time again. "Don't even consider going after her yourself. You would be noticed by the rebels, shot for a traitor before you got within ten paces of the Citadel. Think of what Claire would want. She wants our people to be free more than she wants her life. You have a duty to her. When Shepherd has been deposed, there must be elections, real democracy. Leslie Kantor will not offer those things. She will declare martial law... nothing under the Dome will change except the name of our dictator."

His superior officer was right, of course. Anyone who had seen how Leslie, *Lady Kantor*, comported herself, how she fed zealotry to her rebels in the name of her uncle, would grasp that any power she had at the end of this mess would be amplified by her desires.

She wanted to be a queen, was going to massacre tens of thousands of people to achieve her goals.

Seeing that the Beta grasped where they stood, Brigadier Dane got back to the subject at hand. "Now, tell me Enforcer Corday, is Claire in the east corridor or the basement?"

He didn't know, but he was desperate enough to approach someone who might. "Give me one more day."

Brigadier Dane frowned. "Fine. One more day to make your choice, or I choose for you."

Corday left the woman with his precious data cube so she might study and memorize every last pathway. Hands shoved into his pockets, he walked the streets, squinting from sunlight glaring off dirty frost. Light snow invaded the Dome, crusting everything, the white flakes a sign the glass above them had cracked further.

It was going to be a long walk to the place where Maryanne Cauley hid.

Almost three months had passed since the first time he'd found out just who Claire's old buddy really was.

During a standard reconnaissance mission, he'd seen a familiar face climb the Citadel steps. Blonde braid tied at her back, red lips smirking as if she were the true villain behind it all—the bitch who'd once burst into his apartment looking for Claire had walked right into Shepherd's seat of power.

She was dressed in Follower's blacks.

Corday had waited, sneaking closer. It was hours before she'd left, but when the scamp dared walk down those steps, he shadowed her home. It was easy to track her—so easy he suspected she was *letting* him follow her.

Seeing that woman, one who'd claimed to be Claire's best friend, had stirred up the most sickening hope. After all, it was the Alpha female who'd come to his home looking for their shared acquaintance, who'd had the clothes Claire had last been wearing, who'd claimed that their mutual friend would have traded her life for theirs. Why else would that sneak visit the Citadel, smirking as if bearing a gold embossed invitation to tea?

Everything was about Claire.

He had not approached her then, could not risk the mission by engaging with the female wild-card. All Corday had done was watch her. Now, Maryanne Cauley might be Claire's only hope.

Desperate to uncover any information about his friend's prison, the back of his knuckles banged out three staccato knocks against a traitor's door. A few seconds later Maryanne was there, smirking like a cat about to lick up cream.

The bitch had the audacity to purr at him. "I was wondering when you were gonna come crawling to me. The men always do, you know."

Ignoring the female Alpha's rich vibrations, Corday elbowed past her and barged inside.

Just as he'd hoped, there was a trace of Claire's scent in the cluttered room... one that emanated from the pile of dirty clothes in the corner.

Moving deeper, tracing his finger over lines of furniture, Corday said, “You have been frequenting the Citadel. Why?”

Brushing against him as she moved to the couch, full red lips held a naughty smirk. “I’m a Follower, Corday.”

“Do you always lie? You know I’m an Enforcer. You know where I live... no one has come for me.”

“I survive. You do your thing, I’ll do mine.”

The very tone of her voice revolted him. “Knock off the whole temptress game. That shit is never going to work.”

“That’s too bad,” she chuckled, taking a seat on her couch. “I like pretty Beta boys.”

“I’m sure you hate me as much as I hate you.”

“That would only make the sex more interesting, don’t you think?”

Corday snorted.

“It’s okay,” Maryanne teased. “I can smell Leslie Kantor all over you. Going after the Premier’s leftovers...” She tutted. “You must have a thing for entangled women.”

“I want to talk about Claire.”

The Alpha’s shark smile withered, Maryanne grew deadly serious. “Talking about my dead best friend is the last thing that is going to happen here.”

“When you go to the Citadel, does Shepherd let you see her?”

"Claire is dead, Corday. Move on."

"I know he has her." God, it was hard to admit that out loud. "I have to get her out. If you love her, you need to help her."

There was a look of honest emotion, a deep sadness in Maryanne's lovely eyes. She took a tired breath and sighed. "Claire is gone, Corday. She killed herself. You need to stop whatever madness you're cooking up."

Voice curt, Corday admitted, "If I can't get her out in the next forty-eight hours, she's going to die. Do you understand what I'm saying?"

Maryanne shrugged. "Keep on dreaming lover boy."

He took a seat at the far end of her couch. Elbows on his knees, forehead resting against his clasped hands, he whispered the greatest secret under the Dome. "Leslie Kantor has convinced the rebels to blow up the Citadel. The bombs have already been built. There is nothing I can do to stop it."

There was no reaction from the blonde; it seemed she didn't care.

Corday's scowl deepened, he looked her dead in the eye. "There are only two days left before they strike. Please, just tell me where he keeps her. Tell me so I can save her."

"You're kinda cute when you're delusional. Now, if you'd like to fuck I'm still game." Her sultry voice was back, Maryanne crawling towards him like a playful kitten. "Otherwise, go pester someone else."

Disgusted with the woman and her malice, Corday told her to go fuck herself before storming out of her home.

When he was gone, Maryanne let out a long breath and let her head fall back against the couch. For a second there, she'd been so certain Claire's other lovesick puppy could see right through her act. But she'd done well. Even Shepherd would have to agree, and she was certain he'd seen every last moment of the conversation from the surveillance equipment she knew he'd stashed all over her home.

Now she needed to brace for Shepherd's reaction, because it was clear the psychopath had it bad for Claire and possessed no clue how to properly handle such feelings. Shit, he'd almost ripped her head off when Claire only kissed her goodbye once.

Did anyone appreciate how much she was actually doing to help these resistance assholes? And Enforcer Corday, Maryanne hated his fucking guts, and was keeping him alive when all she'd have to do to assure his slow death was hint that the Omega lived, or warn him that there was absolutely no plausible way to get to her.

But, if what the Beta claimed were true, Corday may have saved Claire simply by opening his big, fat mouth. Shepherd would not expose his mate to danger. Heck, he wouldn't even expose her to anything but plastic cutlery.

Maryanne raised her head and decided she deserved a medal. After all, what if Corday had actually taken her up on the offer to bang her?

Shuddering at the thought, she stood and went to take a very hot shower.

Jules watched the screen, having heard every last murmured insult traded between Maryanne Cauley and Enforcer Corday. Rooted, overlooking several monitors mounted on the Command Center's wall, he issued an immediate order. "Summon Shepherd. Code Red."

The Alpha was at the Citadel, less than five minutes away. That was all the time Jules required to initiate command sequence Exodus.

When his commander arrived, Shepherd watched the recorded exchange; he looked to his second-in-command. It wasn't a ruse on the Enforcer's part; Shepherd could read the pathetic resistance fighter too well. Onscreen there was no scheme or subterfuge. The man believed every word he'd spoken, was disturbed by it. Furthermore, Maryanne Cauley had begun to pace once the Beta slammed the door. Both of them had been infected with what would be dangerous intention.

Shepherd knew the cause of the disease.

Love.

Maryanne, Shepherd could control, but the Beta was going to be a problem. He would have to be disposed of, deal with Claire or no.

There was a throat noise, a grumble, as the Alpha absorbed what was slated in the report. There was only one plausible explanation. Leslie Kantor, *Svana*, was planning this terrible thing.

A fire in Shepherd's eyes, a scent of righteous fury emanating from his pores, he said, "You were right, brother."

There was no vindication upon hearing Shepherd's confession. Jules was above such things. "Svana would plan her strike midday, assuring the majority of your Followers were trapped inside. I estimate she would need less than fifty men if her plan is indeed to demolish the Citadel."

Of course she would plan mass causalities, take out as many of her enemies as she could with one blow; Shepherd had taught her that. It was exactly what he had done when he'd unleashed the prisoners from the Undercroft. "Push up launch procedure. I am calling for an immediate exodus."

"The order was already issued." Jules had to state the risks, the chance of failure. "It will take a minimum of twenty-four hours to ready the ships.

Your men will be scattered, occupied with loading and prepping transport. The Citadel will be exposed, the guard greatly reduced. The Followers might not be able to find all the bombs."

There would be no bombs to find. Svana had always preferred human cannon fodder. What they had to fear, was regular citizens ready to end their lives. "What are the current weather conditions over the Drake Passage?"

Jules pulled up a new screen. "Not favorable."

Shepherd understood the consequences. An expedited Exodus had been discussed and strategized at length. "We will fly over the storms."

"It would take the twelve ships over three days to collect and deposit every last Follower." The Command Center's screens filled with a manifest of soldiers, battle plans, data logs. Jules pointed to the most relevant information. "If Svana stirs up a true rebellion, we may be under siege the entire time, both here, and while annexing Greth Dome. Projected casualties may more than double."

Exactly. Shepherd looked his subordinate dead in the eye. "Then it will not take three days... The final wave of our men will not survive to see freedom."

"Every last one of our brothers understands the sacrifice. All of them would die at your command."

Knowing all of this, Shepherd calculated. "Mated pairs, those who'd recovered their families after the breech will go first. Those in prime reproductive years will follow. The oldest and wounded will remain to defend their brothers' future."

Jules offered, "If we put the Citadel on immediate lockdown, there is a greater chance for our brothers' survival."

"No." Speaking the truth as he knew it, Shepherd warned that Svana was not to be underestimated. "There is a possibility Svana had this planned all along. Our regime removed her every last adversary. She knows the inner workings of our organization. Taking Greth Dome would be more difficult than cutting down our authority. If we let her know before launch that we anticipate attack, she will strike all the sooner. We have to buy our men time."

Nodding, Jules agreed.

"Svana must be detained immediately. Her capture will not stop true rebels from attacking, but we need her alive." Though from the look in his eyes, Shepherd was greatly considering killing her himself. "Enforcer Corday is the key."

"I request that you assign me to track her." There was a darkness under Jules expression, a bloodlust. "I know Svana very well."

Shepherd denied the request. "I need you here, leading our men from the Command Center while I defend the Citadel from attack."

It was very rare for the Beta to question a direct order. "Shepherd, we need her. Without Svana, there is nowhere for our transports to land." Eyes so vibrant a blue they seemed unnatural, Jules asked for something he'd earned over and over again. "Trust me. I will find her. I will hold her accountable to us all."

The future slipping from his fingers, Shepherd conceded. "The instant transports light up the sky, Svana will know her plans were uncovered. You may have less than twelve hours before war begins."

In strategy and war, there was no mental match under the Dome to Shepherd. Jules knew that better than anyone. "You can hold her back, bring the city to its knees. Outmaneuver her men, and save our brothers."

The Dome would have never witnessed such carnage as what Shepherd intended to bring down upon Svana and her rebels. "I swear it to you, Jules."

Jules nodded, wasted no more words, and left Shepherd alone with his guilt and his great obligation.

Thólos was making its death rattle. Shepherd let the fools scrounge up false honor in the eleventh hour, set a shadow perimeter around the

Citadel, and ordered his men to prepare for war. If the rebels' own bombs didn't bring the Dome down on their heads, then Shepherd's vengeance would kill them all.

The virus would be set free. Thólos would be wiped away, and nothing would change that.

Had the Followers no forewarning, Svana may have stood a chance at victory. Now all that would ensue was a bloodbath.

Shepherd would stand as victor.

When the battle was over, when his family was established in Greth Dome, he would be legendary. His success, a thing he had obsessed over once upon a time, would be nothing compared to the new world available for his son and the children who would follow.

There would be peace... after an acceptable period for his mate to mourn, of course. Her breakdown was assumed once she learned the truth, especially as hormonal as she had been lately with the pregnancy.

Claire would not take the frenzy of transport, of flight, and of settling in a new den well if she were unaware of what transpired. Shepherd had agreed with Jules in this, and each man had acted on his own to lay a foundation for her to build upon. Every brick had been fitted together, every hint prepared. All that remained was for Claire to let go of her attachments and willingly choose their son.

Shepherd had absolute faith in her.

His clever Omega knew more than she let on. She was also stronger than she realized. Though Shepherd recognized Thólos had been unhealthy for her for quite some time, his hands had been tied on the matter. But her suffering and unknown sacrifice would lead to great reward. All would be well in the end. He would make Claire happy.

There would be no underground den in her future, only her sky and clean air.

He would find orange blossoms for her.

He would give her anything she wanted, anything in his power once this was over. She would be the most spoiled Omega on the planet, because she deserved it—because even if he showered her with jewels and material things it would never change her character. And there would be children, perhaps even a little Omega girl, like her mother... a girl who would probably boss any Alpha brother about.

But first Thólos had to be destroyed. The world had to be set back in balance so that the woman sleeping in his den stood a chance to survive in it.

His loyal Followers would stake claim to Greth Dome. No soul the wiser as they flourished while the contaminated bones in Thólos bleached in the arctic sun.

A year, maybe two, and Claire would be all smiles. She would see all the benefits; she would forgive, because he knew her secret… he could feel it flowing from her even as she slumbered.

Shepherd smiled.

Chapter 8

"Jesus, Claire, I only took one fry off your plate." Maryanne gawked, wide-eyed, and a little stunned.

Recognizing that she had barked at her friend, Claire took a deep breath, looking sheepish. She was tired, having been woken up and dragged upstairs when all she wanted was more rest. Shepherd had insisted she go see her sky, claimed he'd had special food prepared and Maryanne waiting as company. "I'm sorry, Maryanne. But if you touch another piece of my food, I might have to kill you. I can't help it."

Maryanne snickered, tutting, "Sweet little Claire is all knocked up and nuts. Come on now, show me the baby bump."

Since that painful conversation with Shepherd, everything seemed to keep coming back to the pregnancy... as if he were maneuvering her into a position where she had to speak on it over and over and over. Green eyes looked down at her cotton dress and the tiny bulge that had only just begun to show. "There is nothing to see yet."

A deep, rasping voice ordered from the corner, "Show her."

It was the first time Shepherd had interjected during one of her meetings with Maryanne, and it fed Claire's suspicion. Looking over her shoulder with a pouty scowl, she let out a sigh and stood. Turning sideways and holding the fabric of her dress taut, she made her point.

Maryanne cooed, brown eyes settled on her friend's torso. "You do have a little one! Do you feel anything moving around in there?"

Claire snorted, and looked down at her belly, smoothing the fabric in a small caress before she could stop herself. "What I feel is tired all the time and crazy if I'm hungry... I worry a lot."

"That's nothing new." Maryanne smirked as if trying not to laugh.

Looking at the beauty of her friend, Claire muttered, "I was honestly nicer when I was starving to death than I am when I'm hungry now. I mean look at me. I just threatened your life over a fry. I can't even imagine what other pregnant women in Thólos must be going through."

"Before you sit down, can I touch your belly?" The blonde asked, totally ignoring Claire's mention of Thólos and already reaching out a hand.

It felt very strange to have anyone but Shepherd touch over the infant that was going to be a boy. Claire had not meant to voice her misgivings, they just slipped out as she felt her friend rub the little bump. "It's a strange feeling you know. I can do nothing for this baby..."

Maryanne's hand drew away and soft brown eyes looked to hers. "What do you mean?"

Claire snapped out of her darker thoughts. The damage was done, Shepherd had heard her. "I don't know what I'm going to do. I don't know what I'm doing." She wasn't even sure if she was talking about the baby anymore. Something was very wrong with this meeting, with how hard Maryanne was trying. The whole damn world was wrong.

"Well," Maryanne cocked a little smirk back on her lips. "First you're going to sit down, you're going to take a deep breath, and then you're going to eat the rest of those fries."

Feeling manipulated and cagey, Claire did as she was told until her plate was clean. When it was done, her eyes wandered to the window. It was nearing nighttime, the last of the blue sky peeking between the swollen clouds. Beyond the Dome was the real world, a place she no longer understood, no more than she understood her own thoughts as the hours wore on.

It was obvious that Shepherd, Jules, even Maryanne had been especially obliging lately. And of course, because she felt crazy, Claire's paranoia only grew at their unlikely dispositions. Shepherd had brought her to this room almost every time she'd been awake, listened for hours as she played the piano or just sat with her in the chair, always touching her belly, cupping, stroking, changing his patterns of touch so she could not disregard them and focus on whatever she was doing.

Had the circumstances been normal, it would have been cute—the fanatic Alpha father already bursting with pride... just like her dad had been. She'd lost her temper with him twice for no reason; she just could not stand another moment of being touched. The thing about it that had been most unsettling, was that Shepherd had actually acquiesced.

Then what had the bastard done? He'd pulled out one of his forbidden books... and read to her. And she'd actually liked it!

While he was reading, Claire had glanced at the shelves, Shepherd's *windows*, and glared at the spine of the baby book she avoided like the plague, wondering if there had been some suggestion on soothing pregnancy tactile aggravation with story time. She hated that book, hated that its bright white cover did not fit in with the other books, hated that she was always tempted to look inside, but had to fight herself, to keep distant, because she was afraid.

To stop the whirlwind in her thoughts, she had pressed closer to Shepherd in that confusing moment, sniffing and humming, eyes closed as her hand stroked up his thigh straight towards the distraction she wanted. She'd fondled over the fabric of his cargo pants until he was as hard as she was wet.

Claire O'Donnell had initiated sex.

There was absolutely no hesitation on his end to give her what she wanted, Shepherd going so far as to crawl down as she pressed him lower, her body arching up to silently ask for his mouth. Like a greedy, self-serving woman, as soon as she had come all over his tongue she'd fallen asleep. He must have tucked her in, because when she woke she was deep in her burrow and he was gone.

She had not woken happy... Claire had woken in complete distress.

Shepherd was in a terrible mood again, but that was not her worry. It was that dream, that terrible dream of the Undercroft that seemed to come out of nowhere and wreck her mind—the prisoners foaming at the mouth as they watched through the bars as the devil fucked her.

These horrible phantoms were always reaching; sometimes they touched her and she'd scream.

Sitting up, trying to shake off the chill that followed her out of sleep, her world fell apart. In that moment Claire was certain the gods hated her, that she was cursed. Moving her hand to her belly, she sucked in a breath, and realized there was a sensation she could never ignore or forget. It was the quickening of her baby, the small internal flutter that let her know her son was alive, and that she was a mother, even if she refused to think about him.

When Shepherd found her bawling her eyes out a few minutes later, he had rushed to her, his expression disturbed. Her reaction had been to initiate sex again, and for once he'd responded reluctantly, asking her what was wrong. She'd use her lips to kiss his neck, to mouth the claiming marks, knowing it was manipulative, knowing he would not stop such a thing, but absolutely unwilling to explain what a monster she was.

Since that mating, he'd watched her closely, sniffing her frequently, hyper vigilant. He had a good right to be. He was the father of the baby she had been determined to kill for months, a child that was going to die if she suicided—a baby that existed but did not exist until she'd felt it move.

But now... what was she going to do now?

Claire put away her thoughts and forced herself to focus on the guest waiting patiently for her to speak. Smiling sadly at Maryanne, she asked, "Do you remember the night after my mother was termed a suicide, what the government did?"

"Yeah, why?"

"I'd sat up with my dad that night. He was unusually quiet," the unsmiling Omega began. "We were watching a film when they came banging on the door. Can you imagine how my father reacted?"

Maryanne shook her head in the negative, but watched her friend very closely.

"Our home was comfortable; my mother had flowers flourishing in the windows. I had friends, did well in school, played safely in the causeways. When they came, when orders were given, Dad grabbed me, no questions asked, both of us in our pajamas, and pushed past the Enforcers. His transport had been confiscated, so he dragged me behind him the final distance to the nearest bridge to the next sector. He pulled me so fast I did not even have time to turn around or look back. We went up the elevators, almost all the way to the top of the Dome. The Gallery Gardens... my dad took me to the orange trees before anything bad could touch me. He took me away from the sight of my house being stolen. We stayed in the highest level, for two weeks, some of that time I even forgot to miss my mother. He kept me there until his savings were depleted and we had no choice but to leave."

"That sounds like Collin." Maryanne nodded, unsure what the point of her story was.

"I can't carry my baby someplace where he will be safe. There won't be any orange groves. No playdates in the park, or family vacations." Claire's voice grew darker and slow tears fell down her cheeks. "I cannot even begin to imagine what there will be."

Brown eyes softened and Maryanne said nothing, could think of nothing to offer that would suit. She was not going to lie to Claire and say it would be okay. Her friend was a hunted woman with a mate who had the power to take down the greatest city in the modern world—a man millions of people wanted to see dead. The best she could do was ask, "Have you picked out a name?"

"No."

"Are there any you like?"

"No."

"Well you better pick one. I can see your Alpha thinking Shepherd Jr. is acceptable, and it's just... isn't," Maryanne teased.

Claire offered a tired chuckle, a small twist in her lips before her mouth grew hard. "I tried to kill myself, Maryanne. Shepherd found me preparing to drown in the Thólos water reserve. At this moment, I am only breathing for you. If I had died you would have died, Corday would have died, the Omegas..." It was the first conversation Claire had attempted of that nature in Shepherd's presence, the man choosing not to interrupt. "I did not walk off the ice for my son. Now here I am, alive, and my child is in the hands of a man who is responsible for the genocide of millions and the-" Claire's voice just stopped before she could add, *the mad woman he still kneels to.* Realizing she would have signed Maryanne's death warrant by sharing knowledge Claire knew Shepherd would never allow her friend to walk out of the room with, Claire swallowed and continued, "-the army who follow him."

Narrowing her eyes, nodding, Maryanne looked a little disturbed at the course of conversation. "What are you thinking?"

Reaching for her glass of water, Claire offered, "I am thinking I will name my son Collin, after my father."

Rubbing her crimson lips together, Maryanne looked over her distressed friend and agreed. "Your dad would like that."

A strange feeling came over her. Claire straightened in her chair and spoke bluntly. "I think you should leave now, Maryanne." Standing she gave her friend a sad onceover, "I love you, but I don't want you to come back." Pale arms reached out before Maryanne could react. Embracing her friend, Claire spoke softly into Maryanne's ear. "Shepherd is using you; we both know it, and we both know I can't keep you alive forever. Whatever he wants, don't do it. Save yourself."

When she pulled back and Maryanne's eyes automatically went to where Shepherd approached behind Claire, the Omega sighed and nodded. "You can tell him what I said."

There was something going on between Claire and Shepherd, and at that moment, Maryanne was not sure which one of them was using her more. Claire was making a statement, but Maryanne could not fathom what it was. What she could fathom was that she wanted to get the fuck out of that room and do as she was told.

Claire was eyeballing her with unsettled, tired eyes. "I want to kiss her, Shepherd."

The man behind his mate slowly turned his head to look down at the Omega as if they held some silent communication between them. He did not look pleased. "I will allow it this last time."

Maryanne hardly knew what was going on. Claire stepped forward, stood on tiptoe, and kissed her friend's slack lips. When the small exchange was over, Claire frowned and admitted with a broken heart, "I'm going to miss you more than I can say."

Stepping back to Shepherd, Claire felt his arms circle her middle, his habit of restraining her each time he called for the door to be opened familiar. Shepherd gave the order, and in a matter of seconds, Maryanne disappeared from Claire's life forever.

The table was pushed aside by a thick leg and the chairs brought nearer. Shepherd sat her down, took the seat across, and waited for his mate to meet his eye. "I want you to consider the consequences of what you are thinking right now."

Claire could see it in the link. Shepherd had no idea what she was thinking; he was simply playing the odds.

Engage people with what they expect; it is what they are able to discern and confirms their projections. It settles them into predictable patterns of response, occupying their minds while you wait for the extraordinary moment—that which they cannot anticipate. –Sun Tzu

"I lied to Maryanne when she asked if I could feel the baby," Claire said in a steady, emotionless voice. "I felt him move yesterday... I can feel it even now." Looking back to the window, she parroted what he had said to her weeks ago. "Black hair like mine, maybe my eyes. How many qualities will be paralleled?" The feeling of tears running down her face seemed at odds with her calm tone. "I cannot give him more than an unnatural existence underground. I will not be able to save my son."

Shepherd leaned his mass forward so his elbows rested on his knees and looked pointedly at his mate. "Our son will not be raised in Thólos."

Mirroring his body language, she leaned closer, her voice completely non-reactive, even if she looked like she could kill him. "You will take this child from me over my dead body." Green eyes hardened. "You think you have seen me act out before? What I would do to you if you make one unsatisfactory move against this baby would make you wish you were back in the Undercroft."

"You will never be parted from our children." He answered at once, the Alpha taking immense pleasure in her scathing threat. Shepherd held her hand. "Thólos is not an acceptable place for *either* of you. As such, your departure is imminent."

Claire took a slow breath. "And there is the complication. No one can leave Thólos."

"There is no Thólos. Thólos is gone... it's time to accept that." That big hand moved higher to cup her cheek. "You need to let go and move forward."

"You think I don't know that?" Taking his hand away, running her own over her face to wipe the wetness away, she explained, "I have seen what's happening on the streets no matter the pretty view you provided from this window."

"Then let's embrace the fact our son deserves better. You will live in comfort, be provided for. Paint all day if you wish. I will grant you a piano, teach it to our child." Shepherd was using that earnest tone he employed when speaking of the future, of his plans for the world, all the little promises he had made that she had ignored.

It was making her nervous.

The way his eyebrows lowered at her stubborn expression, the shine of incredulity in his eyes matched the tone of his voice. "Why would you wish to remain here? Why choose the citizens of the city who murder women with dark hair, who are the ones responsible for the deaths of countless innocent children, who turn on each other, climbing like rats on a bloated corpse? How could you possibly be loyal to that over our son? Imagine what they would do to him if they knew who he belonged to."

Squeezing her eyes shut so hard she saw spots, Claire tried to find an answer that made sense. She could not fathom forsaking Thólos even if she had come to hate what it had become—even if everything about a home that she once loved was gone. It was like clinging to the bones of a long dead friend thinking they might one day wake up and hug you back. Grasping at straws, Claire said, "Being parted from the Alpha is dangerous during gestation."

"I would not be parted from you either, little one," Shepherd interjected, his voice holding the trace of a smile hidden in his eyes. "We will travel to our new home together."

Forcing her eyes open, she looked at the set of Shepherd's eyes, dissected his almost eager expression, and did not trust a word he said. "You will leave Thólos, really?"

Shepherd increased the purr, and noticed at once how the sound made her jump and glare right at him. "I am going to leave Thólos... with you."

Clutching at the hand that held hers, feeling a little shaken, Claire demanded, "What of Nona, Maryanne, Corday? What of them?"

He shook his head before his words hissed passed his scarred lips. "Little one, you have to give them up. Aside from Miss Cauley, they believe you are dead. Make peace with it and move forward." Shifting from the chair, kneeling before her, Shepherd wrapped an arm around her middle and cupped her cheek again, his big thumb swiping away the tears. "There is a home for us in Greth Dome; I will give you something beautiful. The best tutors for our children, plenty of unrestrained culture for our family to enjoy..." He spoke honestly, "But, no, there will never be a future in Thólos, or further time with your friends."

Reading between the lines, Claire saw what Shepherd intended towards the people of Greth Dome. "And what of friends for your son?"

He explained simply. "There will be Follower children, and we will create siblings."

Bitterly, Claire asked, "And will this grand home have windows?"

"Many windows with views of distant mountains, and you will be able to move freely through our den."

Claire nodded, finishing Shepherd's thought aloud, "Because it will be on a base full of armed Followers who do your bidding, where I might live locked away from real civilization while you control a new population."

"I will order for a terrace to be cleared for your use as a garden as well." Gently he tried to coax, "You can ineptly kill all the plant life you like."

She felt his urging through the thread, the heated pulse and forthright reassurance. Her attention ran over every part of the man who was offering her a future. But something was very wrong and she could feel it bubbling up inside her like panic. “I need to go outside.”

Liquid iron eyes, hard and serene, sat above a serious mouth. He was not smiling. “No, little one.”

The miasma was choking her. Claire leaned closer to his warmth, needing to smell the thing that was supposed to keep her anchored. He pulled her forward, carefully and slow, to let her settle where he knew she wanted to be, purring louder until his mate’s breathing grew less labored.

Resting her forehead on Shepherd’s shoulder, Claire’s thoughts began to tumble. It should have been horrible to feel such comfort from the man who she should hate, who fed her reassurance through the link, who was going to allow an entire city full of people to cough up blood as they suffered horrific death from Red Consumption.

Her eyes went wide at the thought, her breath hitched, and Claire finally grasped the missing piece as if she had lifted it from his very thoughts. “You are going to release the virus!”

Shepherd did not even blink. “There is nothing but evil here, Claire.”

Frantic, she offered the first word that came to her mind. “Nona.”

"Is a murderer," Shepherd answered. "And it was more than just her husband. Did you know that?"

Eyes welling, she shoved at him. "Do you think I would believe anything you told me?"

He urged her to listen. "Your friend, your mentor, is responsible for the deaths of at least seven Alpha males."

All who probably deserved it, Claire thought. But that was the same argument Shepherd was using towards Thólos. Feeling her expression crumble she tried again. "Maryanne."

Shepherd countered, "You told her to hide. I know what is in her dwelling. If she is wise, she will heed your warning. My men will not interfere."

Claire felt so lost, gripping the front of his armor she knew there was one, one man even Shepherd could not count as evil, one man who had asked her to survive. Heartbroken, Claire whispered, "Corday is a good man."

The Alpha stiffened. "The only civilians who can leave the city are the family of my Followers and newly bonded Omegas."

And she finally understood what he had hinted at for months. "Because the Omegas carry the offspring of your Followers? Because *I am pregnant* with your child..." More tears fell.

"Yes," Shepherd answered softly, kneading the tension where his hands rested on her back. "It was the only way to save you."

The weight of the nightmare fell on her shoulders. Claire slid from her chair. She got down on her knees, mirroring Shepherd's position, but so much smaller, and begged, "Please don't do this. I will do anything you want, bear as many children as you desire. I will love you. *Anything*. Just don't do this."

She had never actually seen the man look desperate. The sound of his breath caught, a quick suck of distorted air preceded his confession, "I cannot stop it; I will not chance an uprising of the scum of this city who may muster, build transport, and threaten our family. Nothing can stop the inevitable." He was already wrapping his arms around her. "Please do not cry."

But she couldn't stop. Nor could she stop how she clung to him as she wept, seeing in the bond the motivation for his deception. It was a pure emotion, acts made from the only good he knew—his absolute love for her. It was the very reason he had inflicted every last horrible thing on his mate, including pulling a syringe out of his pocket and driving a needle into her flesh at that very moment.

Chapter 9

Four precious hours had been wasted in the pursuit and pointless questioning of Maryanne Cauley. Corday had nothing to show for it, no further progress made on his dilemma. On the long walk back to his apartment, outside temperatures grew uncomfortably cold, but the pain of numb fingers was welcome—anything was welcome that might make him feel as wretched as he should.

Hands shaking from the chill, he unlocked his door, his eyes on the spot where Claire had once propped herself up, knocking in the night so he might give her shelter. The smears of blood on her pale skin, the torn flesh, the look of unbearable pain in her eyes, he hated the memory. That's not how he wanted to recall her. Corday wanted to remember her cautious smiles, the spark that would come into her eye on the rare times his jokes chased away the cloud of fear storming inside her.

Had they the fortune of meeting before the breech, Corday was certain they would have been friends, lovers even. Sometimes you just see a person and know... and he'd lost her before she had ever been his.

She'd felt the pull between them too. After all, she had come to him after she'd leapt from the Citadel's roof, ran through the dark and the cold, to reach *him*. He wanted to be there for her, but there was so much she belligerently carried out on her own.

Claire had fought her pair-bond.

Claire had stormed against her mate to free the Omegas.

Through her flyer, Claire made herself a beacon and a movement.

She did it with no support. She did it knowing it would cost her her life.

Releasing a shaking breath, Corday sat back upon his couch, put his head in his hands and, muttered to himself, "Claire..."

Leslie Kantor was a sad shadow in comparison. The Alpha female's fire may have inspired the men and women hidden in the Premier's Sector, she may have successfully reconstructed the resistance into a true rebellion, but she was not eager to sacrifice herself to keep her people safe—not like Claire had been. Instead, she was ready to sacrifice others. Leslie's rebels were fanatical in their adoration of their *gods-sent* leader. Men and women Corday had known before the breech—calm, collected, rational people who'd lost too much, seen too many horrors, had transformed into willing suicide bombers. He hated to even draw the comparison, but his compatriots had begun to behave like disturbing reflections of Shepherd's Followers.

They never questioned, they only obeyed.

They were willing to draw innocent people into the crossfire.

As Lady Kantor would say, that was the price of change.

The sad truth was, no matter the outcome of their attack on the Citadel, unlike Senator Kantor's resistance, the rebels would accomplish something. It might not be the outcome they hoped for. After all, if even one bomb should be incorrectly placed, it could bring down the whole Dome. But revolution would take place. Shepherd and his virus would be eradicated.

New life could be built upon the ashes.

One blast and the stagnation of citizens under the Dome would stop. Riots would ensue; everyone would fight or be killed.

As Leslie loved to say, the people of Thólos were to be reborn.

Corday pressed his palms to his face and tried to rub the nightmare away. Little more than one day was left. Brigadier Dane would carry out her mission, Corday with no ability to know of her success or failure. Instead, he'd be marching with Leslie Kantor.

His former commander expected him to assassinate the leader of the rebels, Dane's reasoning disgustingly sound. Pulling that trigger would most likely cost him his life. He would never see his lovely Claire again. The only thing left he could do for her was to pick the right location of Shepherd's den, so his friend might have a chance to survive.

The words came on a sigh. "The basement or the east corridor?"

From a shadowed corner of the room, an unexpected voice sliced through Corday's concentration. "I'm surprised you would return here, given what you now know. It almost appears as if you want to be captured. Do you, Samuel Corday? Do you want me to take you to Shepherd?"

At the sound of the intruder's taunt, Corday's heart skipped a beat. Breath coming quick, stiff where he sat on his couch, the Beta searched the dark for the source. It was more than fear that churned inside him... it was a strange sense that the intruder was right. Breathless, adrenaline tightening his voice, Corday answered. "I haven't been able to decide."

Again, the toneless voice moved through the dark. "He has a temper. I don't think you would survive a conversation with him. Fortunately for you, whether you tell me the truth or lie, I have no intention of ending your life tonight."

Eyes wide, Corday looked over his shoulder. With so much shadow, he could barely make out the shape of a man—an outline armed with an assault rifle pointed right at him. "What is it that I *know*?"

"You don't know anything but what we've fed you. There is no single fact squeezed into your brain that is wholly correct... And yes, before you ask, Claire *is* alive. Shepherd has nursed her back to health. Four months from now, she will give birth to a boy."

Nursed her? The man in the dark made it sound as if Shepherd were some sweet lover, not the monster who murdered men with his bare hands. Corday did not even try to hide the look of disgust from his face. "After she was captured, Claire exposed the resistance. You've come here to gloat."

"Is that what you believe?" Twisting his smirk with an evil chuckle, Jules took a step out of the dark, exposing his face to enough light that the Enforcer might grasp just who had come. Recognition was instantaneous: Shepherd's second-in-command, the harbinger of death. It was more than the flat expression and lifeless voice, it was the outcast's intention. "She would be so disappointed to hear such a thing from a man she admires as much as you."

The Beta looked heartbroken. "I know she'd never have done it if he hadn't forced her."

"Shepherd's mate has never once offered even a hint of information about you or your pathetic resistance." Face suddenly blank of expression, Jules stared forward with a pair of strangely focused eyes. "It was you who betrayed her."

Confusion darkened Corday's voice. "I would never betray Claire."

Without breaking eye contact, completely aware of how threatening he was, Jules lowered his weapon. "It was you who led me to Claire, you I followed right to the Omegas' hiding place."

Corday knew his eyes were filling, that he could not hide the effect the Follower's words had on him. "Does she know?"

"She's painted a picture of you. You were cooking something in this kitchen, smiling. She left the gold ring you wear on your little finger out of the portrait. I assume she didn't think I'd notice the obvious lack of it." Rifle in one hand, Jules began to stalk from his corner. He walked through the apartment as if the man on the couch was absolutely no threat to him. "She esteems you Corday. Why else would she have promised her life to Shepherd in exchange for yours? And her infatuated mate has kept his word: his men watch over the Omegas, make it so they have access to supplies and clean water without ever interfering with them. You have been left in peace, your rebellion allowed to exist. Even Maryanne Cauley was not murdered for her part in Claire's attack on the Undercroft."

The Enforcer's voice came out, ragged and worn. "Why are you telling me this?"

Lowering his chin to his chest, allowing a subtle sinister curl in his lip, Jules spun a perfect lie. "Claire has asked me to talk to you."

Corday refused to rise to the bait.

Jules taunted, "You lack complete subtlety in your expressions. Five years of torment in the Undercroft would cure you of that weakness. I spent more than a decade underground. What do you think it did to me?"

Corday said nothing. He said nothing because there was nothing to say.

Jules was more than happy to fill the silence. "Many prisoners are quiet in the beginning. If they don't talk, the nightmare isn't real." Jules cocked his head to the side, running his eyes over the Enforcer. "It doesn't take long for them to learn that the nightmare is all that exists. Unfortunate enlightenment leads to despair. Despair leaches away everything else, until a clean slate is all that's left. We were all like you once—silent prisoners. Soon you will be just like me. Leslie Kantor saw your potential and took advantage, she has done well in conditioning you to fit her needs."

There was a thick oppression in the air, a weight that made Corday's body feel immersed underwater. Grinding his teeth until the muscles in his jaw jumped, Corday barked, “What do you want?”

“I don’t like you. You are not a good soldier; you would be an even worse leader.” It was conversational, Jules’s admission. The man even had the audacity to cross his arms over his chest, his deadly rifle’s barrel resting against his shoulder. “The entire city will be caught up in the flames of revolution in a matter of hours, and all you can think about is your selfish need to free one woman instead of trying to protect your people.”

“I will tell you nothing.”

“Keep your plans and your war. There is only one thing I want to know.” Edging closer, Jules let his voice drop to a terrible, grating hiss. “I want to know where Svana is hiding.”

Corday knew that name had been planted on purpose, and could not stop his reactive growl.

Jules did not miss a beat. “Do you love Claire?”

The Beta refused to answer, but his face contorted into an image of fury.

“Do you believe Claire loves you?” Jules pressed, growing more menacing with each word.

The air in the small room seemed to thicken, grow dense with the poisonous hate. The stink was coming from Corday

“Tick tock, Enforcer Corday.” Jules gestured towards the window, pointing to where a fragment of the Citadel could be seen in the distance. “The answers are there. Claire is in there. Are you going to let them die over one woman’s greed?”

Corday shook his head because it could not be true. It was all some trick so he would betray the rebels, too convenient a name to drop. “I have never heard of a Svana.”

“But she has been in this room with you. The very woman who hurt Claire, you have been indulging for months. A lovesick fool who pines after Shepherd’s mate is the exact kind of toy she would have enjoyed the most. Twisting your mind, your memories of so sweet an Omega to reflect what she desired, is Svana’s specialty. I suspect her victory wasn’t hard. You doubt your friend. You believed the woman who saved your life betrayed you, even if it was in a small, coerced fashion.”

Throat tight, Corday’s voice faltered. “Stop.”

“Begging already? But we’ve only just begun.”

A great pain growing behind his eyes, Corday said, “You cannot imagine I would believe a word from your mouth.”

“I’ll confess that you were not under surveillance when Claire must have told you about Svana, so I don’t know the details of what the Omega shared. But, I was with her after it happened, I found Claire laying on the floor. What did you call Svana, a sex-offender?”

There was no point in continuing to pretend that name had no effect on him. Jules had noticed it, and Corday was accomplishing nothing playing dumb. He ground out the words, "Enough! Svana is Shepherd's lover."

"Again you are wrong." There was no hesitation on Jules part to share the secret. "Svana is Shepherd's *partner*... or she was until Shepherd fell in love with an Omega. Now, she is his rival for power."

Corday swallowed the sour taste growing on his tongue, sick with the possibility that the terrible man might be telling the truth. "You make him sound weak."

"Love is an interesting thing." A knowing glow in his eyes, Jules looked pointedly at the Beta who'd made foolish decision after foolish decision all based on his *love* for Claire. "Svana will know we uncovered her betrayal in three hours. Her forces will attack immediately. I am telling you this because I know there is no way to stop them. Even if I kill her, even if you kill her, the slaves she has created will act out her will. Shepherd will be able to mediate a portion of the attack, but bombs will still detonate. How many, I cannot say. So, how will you save Claire?" Unflinching, Jules demanded, "You tell me where Svana is hiding, and I will tell you what Maryanne Cauley would not."

"You have no proof that Leslie Kantor is Svana. I will tell you nothing."

"Perhaps you are right. Sometimes it is best to let storms run their course." Jules smiled, his whole face turned strange with the action. Straightening, he nodded his goodbye. "Claire is kept in the basement: corridor 7, sub-room 3. As the Citadel begins to crumble, she will be crushed to death. Or, if she is really unlucky, she will be trapped under layers of immovable rubble to slowly die from dehydration. Maybe her painting of you will keep her company in the dust and lonely dark."

Once the door was closed and Corday was left alone with his thoughts, he began to shake. It was as if he'd just survived hours of torture, as if just a few soft-spoken words had irreparably damaged him.

Groaning, trying to roll away from whatever was shaking her awake, Claire found her body stiff and numb. Head swimming, it all started to come back. Thólos was going to be turned into a pile of corpses; the Red Consumption would be unleashed. A virus the man sitting at her side, the adoring mate holding her eyes, claimed could not be stopped.

"You have been sleeping for many hours, little one." The purr came strong and sweet. "You must eat now."

The last thing on the planet she wanted at that moment was food.

Claire opened her mouth to complain, only to have a spoonful of something pressed between her lips. Swallowing instinctively, still caught in the fog, she tried to focus on the one man who seemed to blur into two and make him listen.

Shepherd forced more food on her tongue.

"When you have finished, I will help you dress for the journey," That raspy voice was commanding, almost stern, as if he were relaying orders to his Followers. "Then you will be sedated again." A warm hand smoothed back the hair on her forehead. "And next time you wake up, we will be in our new home."

"Please..." Claire barely had time to voice the entreaty before more soup was spooned into her mouth.

"It is important that you eat, or the anesthesia may make you ill. Swallow."

He fought her when she seemed willing to be difficult, rubbing and pinching her throat just enough to earn an automatic response until the whole bowl of soup was gone.

When it was finished, her transformation began. There would be no more green dresses in Thólos. Instead Shepherd outfitted her in the clothing of his soldiers, tugging warm layers over limp appendages, lacing her feet into boots, everything dark concealing fabrics, while Claire lay there, dizzy, and half cognizant from the drugs.

Shepherd kept up a constant stream of what to expect, telling her of the team that would escort her to a waiting transport ship, all explained in a matter-of-fact tone as if she would care.

She didn't.

Even under the influence of drugs, Claire tried to force her thoughts to muster. She tried to think of Thólos, but could only imagine the last things she'd seen in the causeways, dreamed up for the thousandth time the faceless dark-haired women whose bodies littered the streets, the dead frozen boy in the alley, all the Omegas who had gone missing, saw the faces of those who had been left in the city to die.

And what of Thólos, what was left now? The dregs? The worst possible offenders? Would they stand up and fight? Would they evaporate in a burst of blood and wash away everything that had happened here?

This place he was determined to take her, would Shepherd force the people of Greth Dome under the yoke of his *philosophy*? A mess was inevitable, all of it based on the horrible evil that had been done in her city. And if she was dragged away, no one would know of the people who had sacrificed and suffered... so many inspiring stories, stories of good men like Corday, would be lost.

The world needed to know that not everything under Thólos Dome had been dishonorable. Who would tell them?

Refusing to even think for a moment that he might win, Claire stopped all her black thoughts and fisted her hand in the fabric of his sleeve.

Shepherd took her fingers in his, watching her, waiting.

Whatever drug he had given her dulled her emotion, made her listless and rag-like, but she still had the power to accuse, "You gave me your word, Shepherd. On the ice you promised me."

"You were trying to kill yourself, little one. I would have promised you anything," he admitted freely, a hand closing around hers like an anchor, "anything, Claire. You cannot fault me for needing to protect my mate and child. I'd made a mistake, it needed to be rectified. You needed to recover your health and wellbeing in a situation where you no longer had to spend your thoughts on worry for those you count as your friends. You would have done the same had the roles been reversed."

"Is that why you drugged me?"

The man nodded once, placing his huge palm on her belly. “You can be very reactive, and you are very upset. I cannot be with you every moment right now, and I cannot allow you to lash out and harm yourself.”

Claire felt warm tears seep from the corner of her eyes.

Suicide had been her plan, her only recourse against Shepherd: to punish him, to deny him who he would have as mate, to keep his child from him. Yet time had worked on her just as Shepherd must have intended. The baby was more than a blob of cells that made her constantly ill. It was a little moving sign of life... her son. And the man who had created him was at her side, tending her as if she were a dying woman.

But she wasn’t dying and she wasn’t going to kill herself. Shepherd was right; she could never harm her child. And so he’d won the war against her. And Claire knew, deep down, he had won weeks ago. That did not change the lingering fear something very bad would be exacted for his sins.

Claire’s voice broke. “You’re going to lose, Shepherd. I don’t know how, but I know you will. You are going to lose everything in this madness. All your good intentions, all your progress, will have been for nothing if you follow this evil agenda.”

“Now is not the time for arguments. When this is over, when we are established in our new home, grieve your friends if you will. In time, you will see I was right. We stand on the dawn of a new world. Do not be afraid of it, little one. You never have to be afraid again."

She could hardly see straight, but she did try to fight when another syringe was produced and injected into her arm. Then there was no reason to fight, for the world was nothing but strange noisy dreams.

Chapter 10

Out of breath, Corday burst into Brigadier Dane's sleeping chamber, startling the woman awake. The man was wild, doing nothing to restrain his voice. "They know an attack is coming. They are probably listening to us even now."

There was no time for nonsense, Dane furious the man would speak of resistance matters in a room they both suspected was bugged. "What the hell are you talking about?"

"I had a visitor tonight. Shepherd's second-in-command, the Beta, he was in my house." Corday peeked through the blinds, looking for movement outside. "I'm sure he's followed me."

Shoving the covers from her body, Brigadier Dane rushed to dress. "And you led him here? Have you lost your mind?"

Using the meat of his hand, Corday wiped the sweat dotting his forehead into his hair. "You don't understand. He told me where Shepherd is keeping Claire."

She let out a groan, as if she could not believe the stupidity of the man standing before her. "You idiot!"

"Hear me out. Do you recall the name Svana?"

Dane's brow grew tight with thought. It took her a minute to pin it, but she had heard that name. "Half a year ago you reported Svana was the name of Shepherd's lover... the woman who attacked Claire."

"Yes. Tonight Shepherd's Follower offered Claire's position in exchange for the location of this woman. He claimed she'd gone rogue, said she was looking to unseat Shepherd and take his power for her own."

It sounded like a very scary parallel to a woman neither of them trusted. "Tell me you did not betray Leslie Kantor's position."

"I didn't and I don't have to. The man gave me Claire's location anyway. Basement corridor 7, sub-room 3."

Brigadier Dane shook her head. "He lied to you, Corday."

"No." Vehemently, Corday disagreed. "I don't think he did. Look at it from a broader picture. They know the attack on the Citadel is imminent, he told me so himself. He also told me they understood there was no real way to completely stop it. They know you and I are key figures of the resistance, because they *have* been watching us all this time, but they don't know where Svana is. She outmaneuvered them, manipulated us, and I don't have to go where Leslie Kantor hides for Shepherd's Follower to find her. I only have to show up on the front lines, her soldiers will take me straight to their leader."

There was something massive Corday had missed. Brigadier Dane closed her eyes and let out a weary sigh. "If they know rebels are going to attack, the virus will not remain inside the Citadel. All the casualties and structural damage will be for nothing."

Which is why Corday had run here. There was one, terrible option. "If we tell them what we know, we can minimize both of those factors."

It wouldn't work, and Dane was wise enough not to play right into their hands. "If they thought you had any relevant information, the Follower would have taken you. We know they are not above torture. More importantly, Leslie has been clever in compartmentalizing her forces; both of us lack details on the attack."

"I know the intended detonation point of at least six of the bombs. We know the names and faces of the men and women chosen to wear them."

After a moment of thought, Dane was solemn. "If you were to do this, to betray the rebellion, *no matter your reasons*, you are condoning Shepherd's rule. As it stands now, the rebellion still has some power."

"He said Svana," Corday shook his head, clarifying, "I mean Leslie would learn that Shepherd had uncovered her plot within three hours. It took me thirty minutes to get here. In two and a half hours, something is going to happen. What?"

"I don't know." Dane looked miserable, as if she'd wished she'd never woken up. "No matter if she's Leslie Kantor or Svana, don't deviate from the plan. Even with Shepherd's knowledge of the attack, this might be our only chance to free Thólos. Let her attack him... *then do your part.*"

Corday could not help but ask, "What of Claire?"

"If you swear to me you will do as you promised," Brigadier Dane offered her life, on the miniscule potential Claire might actually be saved, "I will find a way to keep our bargain."

"They will know you're coming."

Dane snorted a laugh. "Thanks to you, they know we're all coming."

Before the two might find comfort in their mutual agreement, the ground shook. It was a slow moving rumble, one that grew louder, almost deafening. It was not the distant boom of detonation that made such a racket, it was the following roar of bending metal and screams of falling glass.

Dane threw back the blinds, her view of the disaster sucking the breath from her lungs. "No!"

The Citadel had not been the source of the blast. Someone had detonated explosives right against the glass of the Dome. The East and West sky were caving in.

"It's too soon..." The words were spoken with such disbelief that shock appeared on Shepherd's face. "Svana has discovered we are prepping to launch."

When the unexpected blast had torn girders and solar power collection plates from their moorings, Shepherd had watched from the Command Center, calculating as damage reports flooded in. There was no denying what they saw. Rebels had purposefully shattered two massive segments of the Dome's protective glass. Shepherd, the Followers gathered in the room, stood there, while the northeast and southwest barrier wall crumbled. The city was turned into one giant wind tunnel.

Svana had altered the battlefield.

Turning to the Followers gathered behind him, Shepherd did not hesitate to counter her move. "Lock down the Citadel. Broadcast a fallback order and shut down communications and power to every segment of the Dome outside this building."

Watching the monitors, an outside change in air pressure was already sucking out huge gusts of debris. A soldier diligent at his post warned, "Shepherd, with catastrophic failure of the Dome, the temperature in the city is rapidly dropping. If we divert power from the Dome's heat generators, our men outside will freeze to death."

Under incredulous brows, Shepherd's eyes burned. "They won't have time to freeze to death."

The soldier didn't understand, "Sir?"

"This was not like an attack against the Citadel, their *enemy*. This was an attack on the population. Panic will ensue... riots. Cutting their power will slow them down."

Typing furiously across the Command Room's console, another soldier interjected, "Sir, I cannot shut down the communications network. The fallback order has not been sent."

"What is preventing it?"

Frustration was palpable in the man's voice. "Someone has taken control of the system."

A message began to roll across the screen: *People of Thólos, the rebel forces are in possession of the virus. Storm the Citadel, destroy our enemy.*

There was a blended murmur of curses offered up once the soldier read the lie. It was brilliant and also painfully devious. Svana had openly just betrayed every last Follower who had sworn an oath to install her as queen of Greth Dome.

Shepherd didn't have time to roar out his anger. Not now. "Get the first wave of transports ready to launch. Ship 7 must remain until Svana has been captured and stowed onboard. Have our men build a fire around it to keep it warm."

A young man who had survived the torment of the Undercroft thanks to Shepherd, looked to his commander and acknowledged that he could not carry out the order. "They need another hour, sir."

Shepherd impatiently detailed the outcome should they not get those ships in the air. "If the transport ships' engines freeze, they will seize. Successful launch will be impossible. Svana is attempting to cut off our exit." He had more orders to give. "Bridges linking the Citadel to the city must be destroyed. That will remove at least seven access points to our gates. That leaves only the promenade before the steps. We will funnel the citizens into that arena, and kill them before they can storm our walls."

"Yes, sir."

"I will return in an hour." Shepherd looked to his COMspecialist and barked, "By that time, I expect you'll have regained control of the communications network and disrupted the rebel's message."

"Yes, sir."

Shepherd looked to leadership gathered in the Control Center and said what they were all thinking. “We fight for our brothers now. If we can hold the rabble back for twelve hours, if we can keep the Citadel and the transport pad intact, they will live the life we’ve dreamed of.”

There was a cheer, a lack of desolation. Every man in that room was more than willing to die for his brother.

Shepherd left them to carry out their orders, the expression of detachment and ruthless focus he had maintained for his men falling away the instant he was running to his mate through the underground catacombs.

Jules had sworn to him he would do his duty and gather Svana. His men would lock down the Citadel and destroy as many access points as time would allow. Now all Shepherd could manage was one hour before he had to send his mate to a future where more and more it seemed he would be unable to follow.

All he could do was buy time.

It would not be enough... not for the seventy-two hours it would take before the third round of Followers might be rescued.

The groaning of their metal door did nothing to stir the beautiful woman sleeping in her nest, and for one minute Shepherd allowed himself to just look down at her, to pretend he would get to enjoy that vision every day as they grew old together.

Long black hair streamed over pillows in what Shepherd had learned was a shade called bird's egg blue: her favorite color. She looked so peaceful in sleep, the fan of her lashes lowered to pale cheeks, her lips gently parted, and of course, her little hand resting over their son. At the upcoming moment of his death, that was the image he would carry to the grave.

Taking a seat on the bed, he pulled Claire to his lap and cradled her. He held her in the same manner in which she would cradle their child once Collin was born. Shepherd did not miss the parallel, tracing his favorite parts of her face and trying to memorize this last peaceful moment.

There was no other time in Shepherd's life he could recall a handful of minutes as being so precious.

Time in the Undercroft had dragged by, moved at the grating pace of skin slowly scraped over broken glass. There were days it had been almost unbearable, and it drove many prisoners mad within a few years.

Since Svana had guided him from that hell, time had taken on a quality of almost moving too fast. There was never enough of it, always so much to do, hours that needed to be dedicated to training, to planning.

All of that had changed the instant he'd seen Claire.

Time affected him differently in her presence. One soft look from her felt like an eternity—one of joy not tedium. She had breathed life into him, restoring whatever the Undercroft had claimed before Shepherd had even been the wiser he'd been deprived.

In that moment, holding her as she slowly woke from his gentle prodding, an hour was not enough.

Regret was not a sensation he was accustomed to, but as he held her on his lap and called for her to wake, to open her eyes so he might see them one last time, he intensely regretted a great many things.

"Look at me, little one." By the fourth or fifth time he called to her, her lashes parted and glassy green, his favorite shade of green, was there for him to smile at. "I need you to wake up just for a little while."

Her pupils seemed to focus enough to express he had her attention as she fought the drugs and whispered his name. "Shepherd..."

"Little one," Shepherd beckoned, "Listen closely. I have to send you away, and I cannot go with you now." The man felt pressure building behind his eyes when the look of alarm widened hers. "There is a team prepared to escort you to your new home. I will do everything in my power to follow after you, if I can. In case I cannot, an Alpha, his name is Martin, was chosen by me to act as surrogate until our son is born. He is a good man. You will approve of him."

"NO!"

"I am sorry." Shepherd heard his voice crack for the first time in his life. His shoulders shook, breath difficult as her tried not to frighten the pleading woman.

Drops of fluid fell from him and landed on her when she grabbed the lapel of his jacket and pulled their faces closer together. "Shepherd," Claire knew this was not a nightmare no matter how dreamlike the drugs made it feel. She struggled not to slur as she spoke to her grieving mate. "Whatever she has done to force you, just say no. Leave with me now. Chose me, chose your son... and wash your hands of this. It's not too late." She sobbed in earnest, kissing him as she begged. "Please."

"I love you, little one, but I cannot leave. I have a duty—"

"To me!" Claire cried her arms circling his neck, holding onto him with all her strength. "To our son!"

Lips at her ear he tried to explain in a rushed whisper, "Even if I were to leave and abandon my men, I would be a labeled a traitor. Before our ships might even land, you would be slaughtered. You have no idea how powerful this army is, how far each member is willing to go. The only way I can make things right, is fight here so that you and Collin can live."

His armor was between them, dampening the purr he projected as loudly as he could. Even so, Claire kept pressing closer. Her mouth was on his mark, her tongue swiping up the salt of his sweat.

He knew what she wanted; he wanted it to.

Shepherd pulled off one of her boots, tugging her leg free from clothing so that his mate could climb to straddle him. She wrapping around his body as if she might actually possess the strength to reject his verdict and hold him there. As he caressed her bare buttocks, she reached between them to set his member free. Lowering to accept him, she begged him to stay with her, sliding her body down with no urging from his hands, until he was sheathed root to tip.

He told her he loved her so many times he lost count, brushing his lips over hers, feeling her clench as he rolled his hips up to meet her warm internal embrace. With desperation on both sides, far more wrapped up in the press of their lips, in the war of searching tongues and shared breath, than even the act of mating, each of them tried to communicate why things must be their way.

Shepherd's hands were buried in her hair. She never once stopped kissing his face, feeling the wetness on his cheek, unsure if it came from her or him. When she came, it seemed almost too soon, and Claire tried to fight it until he murmured, “Please.”

Moaning his name against his lips, calling to her Alpha, climax rolled over her no matter the despair. “*Shepherd...*”

Shepherd held her tighter, his body shaking with the plea. “Please... just tell me once.”

Even as the waves of pleasure filled her with warmth in her core, even as she felt sexual gratification, her voice broke, and with hitched breath, she met his eyes and sobbed, “You already know I love you.”

His release came, paired with a man pulling in a breath as if it was his first. He looked at her with undying devotion, liquid iron eyes memorizing every last detail of her tender expression, of her heartbreak.

Through the entirety of the knot, Shepherd touched her as if she could not be real, kissing every part of her face. Petting, stroking, as if the memory of her flesh was something he could carry with him if he just caressed a little longer, lingered a little more.

The mating, the purrs, the worshipful touching, blended with the power drugs. Before he could leave her womb, his Claire had fallen back into the slumber of her drug-induced sedation. He embraced her so powerfully she would be bruised, so that when she woke up and he was dead, she would know he had been with her.

Aware time was short, he placed her folded portrait of him into her jacket's inner pocket, the back of the painting covered in a hastily scribbled note. Her clothing was righted, boot returned to her foot and laced. Then there was one final thing he told her, a thing he had never once said in his life to anyone else but her, not even to Svana. He told her again that he was so very sorry. And then he whispered the name Claire had chosen for their son; he called to Collin while palming the small sign of life and said the same to him.

With not even a minute to spare, Shepherd hoisted her up and carried her to the elevator where a hand-selected team waited to escort his mate and heir out of hell. Amongst his brothers stood the Alpha surrogate Jules had suggested weeks ago: Martin, a man who had stood outside his door for months on guard... a surrogate Shepherd had approved, though he hated doing it.

Handing her over to another man, even one as respected as the Follower standing before him, was almost impossible. Not killing that man when Shepherd's red eyes viewed Claire in his arms was even harder. Martin had read her dossier, he knew what to expect and what Shepherd's orders were in regards to how she must be treated—like a queen.

Looking the man dead in the eye, Shepherd snarled, all traces of softness gone, "She is going to be exceptionally difficult when she wakes. If she refuses food, force feed her if you have to. Do not allow her to harm herself in her temper. Should it reach a point where she is out of your control, and it will, explain to her that I told you to call her a little Napoleon. She will be shocked, she will cry, and then she will calm down."

The Follower nodded his understanding. "Yes, sir."

Shepherd cocked his head, signaling that they must close the door and make their way to the Citadel's launch pad.

As the elevator door rolled down between them, Shepherd caught it with one darting hand and leveled the full power of his intimidation on the surrogate, adding, "Under no circumstances are you ever to strike her."

"I understand, brother," Martin answered, stoic yet honored. There was even a spark of compassion in his eyes. "I will treat her as if she was my own."

Shepherd dropped the door and knew it was over. As he walked back to Command, he counted down the seconds like a madman. He knew exactly how long it would be to launch, the exact amount of time before Claire would be airborne.

She'd teased him for that skill time and again.

Back at Command Center, he felt the first building tremors of the launch, video confirmation showing eleven glowing ships lighting up the pre-dawn sky over the broken glass of Thólos Dome.

Stage one of operation Exodus had been a success, and even though the men left behind stood little chance of survival, they cheered for their brothers who thrived.

Shepherd sighed and refocused on the problem at hand, unaware Claire had never made it to the ships.

Svana had made certain of it.

Chapter 11

Maryanne Cauley had everything she needed: generators, enough fuel to last her for years, food, water, clothing, medicine—everything a person might need to survive the apocalypse.

Tucked safely in her sanctuary, she could hear the wind howling like a freight train outside, and chose to ignore it. Huddling next to a heat source, she kept the lights off, so no other soul might realize she had power when they had none. There was no reason to peek out her window or unbolt her door, her COMscreen told the tale of what was going on outside. The Dome had been purposefully ruptured. The networks had gone wild, computer viruses plaguing every last corner.

She knew how to work around them.

The hacks were inexpert, yet so numerous that it took her some time to recognize that Shepherd's men were not responsible for the disaster. In fact, she could see that they had their hands full trying to clean up the communications mess.

One dangerous message continuously rolled across her screen:

People of Thólos, the rebel forces are in possession of the virus. Storm the Citadel, destroy our enemy.

Another series of blasts went off in the distance, small little pops that made Maryanne jump.

So, who the hell was attacking the Dome? Who else did she have to contend with?

That prick, Corday, had said the resistance was going to attack the Citadel. That made sense, even if it was pointless. Why bring down the glass encasement that kept them all alive instead?

This would lead to more than a coup. The entire city would panic, there would be riots.

Shepherd would be blamed. Whoever had done this wanted to start a war that no one could win.

Between the icy wind and the unmitigated violence, between the possibility Shepherd would release the virus, everyone would die.

Wrapping her arms around her body, her knees tucked under her chin, there was a strange internal stirring Maryanne wanted to ignore. A smattering of shame knocked about in her breast.

She knew what the panicking city did not. The only thing in store for those who rose up against Shepherd was a bloodbath.

Unless...

No. It was not possible, and she owed this city nothing. The only soul she gave two fucks about was Claire. Her friend had told her to hide; Maryanne was going to listen to her.

But, maybe she could just fiddle around, take down that message, and reopen the communications network. After that, she was done, no more. Screw Thólos.

It took time to unravel the mess, to outthink whoever was responsible for hijacking the networks, the more Maryanne disrupted their work, the more she understood what they were really doing.

It was fucking horrible, sloppy even, as if there was no concern for the consequences. For that reason alone, Maryanne continued to ghost her cyber-attack right against their gates. Sneaking behind their firewall, she found something she could not wrap her head around.

The rebels were the party responsible for ruining the Dome; it was their chatter back and forth that showed units spread all over the city working in unison to stir up riots. They were using the very civilians they claimed to be fighting for as human war fodder.

For all her flaws and selfishness, even Maryanne was disgusted.

Because she felt like a salty bitch, and because she could, Maryanne seized control of the networks completely and shut the whole fucking thing down. She might not be able to save the idiots of Thólos, she didn't even really want to, but she could offer an alternative.

She set up a new message to stream over and over.

The only safe place is underground.

Knowing what was down there, what was up here, Maryanne was not sure if she had offered mercy at all.

A nausea inducing feeling of vertigo broke through Claire's stupor the instant a hard smack landed against her cheek. Blinking, confused at the circles of lime deposits she saw on an unfamiliar ceiling, she tried to touch her head and found her hands bound together, stretched above her body and fixed to something she could not pull away from. As she struggled, a beautiful face came into view—a beautiful face belonging to an incredibly evil woman.

Even with the drugs in her system, a feeling of terror brought ice to Claire's veins from one simple sight of those psychotic eyes looming over her again. Careful to keep her face blank, to not give the woman the pleasure of feeding off her fear, Claire nodded and said, "Hello again, Svana."

"Hello, pretty one." Svana gave a small, knowing smile, a facsimile of the smile that had played on her lips when her hands had circled Claire's throat months ago. "I see you've been studying Jules's art of expression."

Claire felt a chill creep over her skin, and it was not only brought on by fear. She was cold because all her clothing had been removed, and the cot Svana had put her on was bare of blankets. Instead, it was covered in blood stains and stank of foulness.

"I can't play with you for too long. You see I have plans to visit someone I am very much looking forward to seeing." A long fingernail traced lightly from the valley between Claire's breasts and down her belly, Svana insincerely admiring what was beneath her. "But the gods gave me this time with you, and I will not waste it. Martin, the others, did not even question when the elevator doors parted on the fourth floor. Why would they question their savior? I shot them so quickly, I am surprised there is not more blood on you… but, it won't take long before you are covered in it."

"You do realize you are giving me what I want?" Claire offered a challenging gaze, forcing her body not to tense when that nail scraped over her child. "I could not live without my mate anyway. It is fitting we die together."

Svana purred, lightly tracing a circle over Claire's mound. "Then I will allow you to thank me."

Claire spat full in her face.

The look of disbelief, the instant rage that someone would dare such a thing, was something Claire was only able to enjoy for a moment before Svana reached up to wipe the wetness from her cheek with her sleeve.

"You know what I have learned, little one?" Svana giggled under her breath, her tongue darting out to lick at the spittle nearest her lips. "It's to let the men always underestimate you. Let them think you are flawed, that you need them. Do you have any idea how many times I have stood in your room and watched him fuck you? Neither of you knowing I was near enough to touch. When your eyes were closed, when he buried his face in your neck, sometimes those fingers carding through your hair were mine."

Claire's mask cracked; it was impossible to keep the revulsion from her face. Feeling Svana chip away at the little courage she could manage, the Omega knew in that moment the exact type of wickedness Shepherd spoke of when he spoke of the true evil that had been cast in the Undercroft. It was all there, a conglomeration of vileness in the woman running her nail up and down the slit where Claire was still slippery from Shepherd's last ejaculation.

"It has been unpleasant, the way things have gone," Svana pouted, her mouth heading towards a cold tightened nipple. "But I have done

Shepherd a favor in this. You are a whore, desecrated and as disgusting as this city—unworthy of a man like him. But like all men, he is weak." That single finger slipped easily inside Claire, no matter how her muscles clenched to deny her entry. "They all bow to this. Premier Callas, Shepherd, even my dead uncle. It's a pity I was not born Omega, I would have ruled the world ages ago."

Once the initial penetration had passed, Claire did not fight; she lay passive knowing Svana desired her resistance. Drugged as she was, she had no energy to fight, had extreme difficulty even focusing her eyes, and embraced the wave of chemical euphoria over the terror of what was taking place.

Swallowing back a shriek, unwilling to cringe when the hated woman lapped at her nipple, Claire lay still and fixated instead on her son's fluttering movement deep inside her. Everything else was shut off.

"Now," Stroking Claire's black hair affectionately, Svana smiled as if they were old friends, still pumping in and out of the Omega's body, "I won't be able to stay and watch. Far more important things than you require my attention."

With a lingering kiss on Claire's mouth, a little flick of the tongue forced between her lips, Svana pulled her fingers from Claire's body, licked them clean, and made her goodbye.

"I want you to know," Claire called to Svana's back before the woman exited the cell.

Svana turned, eager to hear the Omega beg, "Yes, dear?"

It was not even difficult to say, "I want you to know that I love him. That even after everything, I learned how to do it. And that is something you could never achieve."

Svana laughed as if the very concept were absurd. She stood a moment, taking in the view of her enemy bound and at her mercy, the tip of Svana's tongue licking over the edges of her teeth. One more chuckle, and she opened the barred door, leaving Claire naked and bound on a musty bed, while three men covered in Da'rin markings entered, smiling and eager.

Claire knew what was coming; a monster like Svana would require degradation and horror before death was achieved. Claire could smell the two putrefying corpses piled up in the cramped cell's corner, could see from the withered limbs and small frames that the poor woman had been Omega.

Death was coming for her. Death was coming for her baby. And it was all there in the smiles of the Alpha outcasts who circled like sharks.

The instant the first one touched her, Claire knew she would not be able to hold back her screams for long.

Brigadier Dane had to fight her way through the mob clogging the tunnels. The streets were chaos, having made it hard enough to get close to nearest underground access point, but navigating underground through the confused throngs was almost impossible. Some of the city was wise; a portion of citizens chose not to engage in the war, but to retreat to the Undercroft, away from the bitter cold already leaching the life from the city.

Or they were just plain cowards.

The farther Dane moved underground, the more she believed the latter. From all directions, a cacophony of voices, of screams, wails, and outright shouting was so loud, was amplified so greatly by the tunnels, that Dane could palpably feel the tremors of their fear

She'd only stomached it for less than an hour. This place had once been crammed full of tens of thousands of castoffs. What would five years trapped in the Undercroft do to a mind? It would unhinge a person, that's what it would do.

She wanted out, but the only way out was up. Even with a COMscreen projecting the data cube's maps, often she'd have to guess when she found a newly carved out juncture. The ant farm Shepherd's men had carved was a maddening circle designed to trap the unwelcome. The paths made no sense; every direction led her back to the same place.

That had to be why so many were screaming; they were lost.

Behind the heavily barred door she'd strained to force open, Brigadier Dane saw the first one. A man little more than bones, his body covered in the repulsive, telling marks of Da'rin. He rushed at her from the dark. Reaching for her weapon, she'd fired without thinking. It was not until after he'd collapse, she realized her hand was shaking.

The Undercroft was getting to her.

The corpse lay crumpled, gripping a shiv, hardly a rag covering his body.

There were more of his kind, she found them around almost every turn. Most shrank from her, from the light of her screen. They cowered against the walls and wept, as if she had come only to cause them pain. Some tried to stalk her through the twists and turns. Fortunately for Dane, she had more bullets than they had life to spend.

These men were never supposed to be set free. Shepherd had left them here for a reason.

Saturated in the stink of human waste, of things far more rotten than any corpse aboveground, Dane plodded forward. She went North, always North. It took an hour to reach the gate she assumed must block this sector from the city center.

All that metal, all those gears and locks, someone had thrown them open.

Sniffing the air, Brigadier Dane hesitated. Something was not right. The citadel was on the other side of that door, of that she was certain, but the smell of Omega was here.

The sound of screams, the very horrible music she had been subjected to. Dane began to listen.

She heard a sobbed name buried in the noise. Someone was screaming for *Shepherd.*

Corday could hardly believe what he was a party to. The rebels had done enough damage that outcome of the battle aside, millions would die from exposure. Subsequently, just by coming to this place, he had betrayed the resistance. Everyone was doing harm to everyone else.

There was no *right* path. Not in Thólos.

It was so cold his fingers were losing feeling, the rebels around him buried under layers for warmth—because, unlike him, they had known what to prepare for.

It was as Brigadier Dane had said: Leslie had purposefully concealed the details of her battle plans from the pair of puppets she used to distract Shepherd's men.

What else had she hidden? Was it as Shepherd's second-in-command claimed? Was she Svana?

Had she been the one who'd assaulted Claire all those months ago?

The seed of doubt had burst and blossomed. It was hard to admit, but Corday *believed* the Beta who'd invaded his house, and he hated himself for it.

He had helped the woman seize power. He had helped her plan, gathered items used to craft the very bombs that had shattered two segments of the Dome. She had used him, and he had come to where the rebels mustered, knowing Shepherd's second-in-command was still out there somewhere, watching him.

"Where is Leslie?" The words came in a rush, Corday pulling his body up the last segment of the ladder. The roof before them held ten men, Leslie's men, all standing atop their perch, watching the city devour itself.

"We were told to hold position." A man grizzled in appearance and unruffled by the situation said, "Lady Kantor will arrive once her mission is complete."

"What mission?"

Jaw covered with a red, bristled beard, the man turned his eyes to Corday, and said nothing.

His reply, it was something Dane would have barked. Mouth in a firm line, Corday chastised a man who'd only recently been recruited, "I will remind you of your rank in our forces. While you were warm and fed, protected in the Premier's Sector, I was running missions, risking my life so this day might come."

There was a brief instant the man's composure slipped. He stood abashed. "Her mission was classified. We don't know where she is. All communications went down twenty minutes ago, so we wait. Chances are, she moved to another position."

As if it were his place to command, Corday pointed to the youngest in the group. "You, climb down and run to the team at sector G. If she is there, update us immediately."

"I am afraid that man already has his orders, Corday."

Corday rounded, looking for the source of Leslie Kantor's voice. She had snuck up right in the midst of their collective, not one of them having heard her crest the roof. "Leslie?"

She smiled to see him, remaining at a distance. "Our plan is advancing exactly as expected. Every rebel was prepped and knows their duty. The disruption of the communications network changes nothing."

His fingers were so close to the gun holstered at his hip. "Leslie, why didn't you tell me our men were going to blast holes in the Dome?"

From the absolute steadiness of her expression, it was obvious Leslie had been prepared for and unconcerned by the question. "The airstream surrounding the Citadel is a countermeasure in case Shepherd unleashes the virus before our bombs might cleanse it from existence."

The virus was airborne, heavy winds would only spread it faster. Her excuse was so lacking in substance, that Corday could not contain his feelings of despair. "Without protection from the elements, it will grow uninhabitable in the city. You've condemned our people to the Undercroft."

"Really, Corday... you can be so dramatic." Waving him off, Leslie marched to the edge of the roof, assuring the only way Corday might hear her continued explanation was to follow at her heels like a dog. "Yes it will be difficult at first. Given the state of manufacturing and resources, projections show it will take four years to repair the damage. In the meantime, citizens unnecessary to the immediate reconstruction of the Dome will be *safe* underground. Those key to the effort of restoring our city will find sanctuary in the Premier's Sector."

Some would live in grandeur and luxury while others wasted away in the dark. "I see."

She hesitated, looked him in the eye. "This was the only way to ensure change. Sacrifice must come from all of us."

And what was she going to sacrifice?

He hated her in that moment. Even so, he nodded as if he understood. Staring down at the madness, Corday found that the number of angry citizens circling the Citadel had increased, compacting into a single waving mass working to reach the steps.

Followers were shooting at them like fish in a barrel.

They were dying for nothing, in fact they would all die should Leslie's bombs detonate. Cutting a glance back to the smirking woman at his side, he knew she saw his distrust. It seemed pointless to continue his charade. After all, he'd already condemned them all.

Corday's lip almost shook when he asked. "He told me your name is Svana. Is it true?"

The corners of her mouth curved up from smirk to smile. Impudent, she asked, the question coming out as absolute confirmation, "Who?"

Behind them a rough edged voice rang out. "It's time, Svana. Shepherd has sent me. He wishes to negotiate the terms of his surrender."

Like Leslie, he'd appeared with no sound.

No longer was Shepherd's minion dressed in the blacks of Followers. He looked like any other civilian. Or he would have, if he didn't have such a massive firearm resting in slack arms.

Turning her back to the carnage below, Leslie held up her hand, signaling to her men all was well. Once they had lowered their weapons, she offered a twisted greeting. "Jules, I expected you sooner. Hasn't this gone on long enough?"

Seeing him in the daylight, Corday found the Beta to be only a ghost of a person. There was something wrong with the way his eyes tracked their movement, a lifelessness to his face. When he spoke his voice was not only disinterested, it was dead. "It has."

"Fine." Leslie nodded, crossing her arms over her chest. "Kill these men, and let's make our way."

Before the word *kill* had crossed Svana's lips, the Beta acted. In a blur he'd shouldered his rifle and showered a spray of bullets on Leslie Kantor's bodyguards. As the untried rebels fell, only two had squeezed off return fire before their death—a single bullet embedding in the concrete at Jules's feet.

Lowering his weapon, he scowled at the woman, disgusted by the men's utter lack of skill when it came to actual combat. "You did not train them well."

Leslie ignored the taunt. Instead, her focus was on where Corday lay. The impact of a bullet had knocked him down, a growing bloodstain marking his thigh. Rattled breath twisted his groans. One hand to his wound, he scrambled to lift his weapon.

All it took was Leslie's foot atop his wrist to stop the pathetic attempted attack.

Reaching down to take Corday's gun for her own, she complained. "He's still alive."

Jules's answer was dry. "Shepherd desires that this one suffer."

"Poetic." Pointing his gun at his skull, the woman seemed to debate the benefits of letting Corday meet a cold, lonely death on the roof. Maybe it was the way he cursed her name over and over. Maybe it was because he had been her plaything for so long. Either way, she took a step back. "Fine. I will give Shepherd this one last concession."

On the edge of the roof, standing confident and free, she cut a glance at the Follower and explained her deeper thinking. "He forced my hand, you know. This wasn't how I wanted it to be. Shepherd made me do this. You understand that, Jules."

Jules stared down at the panting man, took a long look at his handiwork, and curled his lip. "I gave you your chance to shoot her. You hesitated."

The smile Svana wore, the self-assured cocky smirk, diminished to the point where her face was blank, chilling. "You would dare insult me now? Not one of you—"

Jules didn't acknowledge a word out of her mouth. Before she could make any grand speeches, he unloaded ten bullets into her chest.

Eyes bugging out of his head, Corday struggled to scoot out from under Svana's collapsing body. "What the fuck?"

Jules ignored the inconsequential Beta, choosing instead to tower over Svana's pretty bleeding corpse. "After some recent thought on the subject, I disagree with Shepherd. I don't believe we need you alive to take Greth Dome. We only need parts of you to bypass scans—a hand, some blood, maybe an eye. The rest of you is garbage that we will harvest at need. Enjoy your legacy."

Reaching down, he hoisted the woman across his shoulders, hesitated when her body brushed his face. He crinkled his nose in a deep sniff, and growled once the trace of fading scent registered. His face contorted and he looked as if an ocean of profanities were rising up to his tongue.

As quickly as the rage began, he shut it off.

Jules swallowed, and once again became an empty, hollow thing. Svana bleeding all over him, he glanced once to where Corday grew pale, slumped against the roof's retaining wall. The Enforcer was dismissed with one derisive glare before Jules climbed down from the roof with his prize.

He left Corday alive.

Chapter 12

The grand doors of the Citadel wide open at his back, the city in shambles at his feet, Shepherd looked over his dying kingdom. Sun sinking over a broken wasteland, aging light stretched shadows atop the sea of Thólosen men and women desperately trying to reach their tormentor. His men had done well disrupting pathways by destroying bridges and hastily constructing barricades. The unwise that approached, had only one plausible path to his doorstep.

To his loyal Followers armed on the overlooking fragmented causeways, he ordered, "Fire at will."

A wave of gunfire erupted, an upsurge of enraged citizens falling under the stampede of their rabid neighbors. More protestors climbed over the growing hill of the dead—like locusts they kept swarming, hour after hour.

All Shepherd could do was clog the path, and keep the masses, and Svana's bombs as far from the Citadel as he could.

He had broken down the odds, added up all known variables. Soon those desperately trying to climb over the dead would be hungry and thirsty. If he were lucky, they would make it until nightfall, where violent winds barreling through the Dome might drive Thólosens to seek shelter in the Undercroft, as every COMscreen under the broken Dome suggested. But the colder it grew, the more arrived in mass to shout and throw things across the divide separating the Citadel from the city.

There was a greater unresolved issue beyond the insects gathering at his doorstep: Svana

She was yet unaccounted for. The ships that had already launched would be stuck hovering out of range of their intended target until they had their key to Greth Dome in hand. His men, his mate, would be trapped out there just as he was trapped in here, if Jules failed to find her.

Until she was delivered, those same ships would not be able to return and gather the army waiting for freedom. Unless the transport ships returned soon, a second round of evacuations would be impossible.

There was no hope left for those deserted in Thólos. His men knew it.

Should Shepherd have the opportunity to lay eyes on Svana again, he would be hard pressed not to reach out and tear her limb from limb.

Claire had been right; he had created a monster in Svana just as she had harnessed the violence in him. As a team, they had been unstoppable. As adversaries... they knew one another so well, it was like fighting against one's shadow.

Moves and countermoves, and they were still at an impasse. She knew he would not unleash the virus so long as there was even a chance his men might survive. That's why she'd given it to him, a final taunt he'd been too foolish to recognize.

Even armed with the greatest weapon in history, he was powerless.

She held control, her absence aside.

He'd put her on that untouchable pedestal himself. In tormenting Thólos, he'd created for her the perfect fodder to fling at his wall. Svana knew what to look for in the hearts of men, and had used her experience to her ultimate advantage. Worse, she had done it right under his nose.

Jules, Claire, had both tried to warn him.

No matter the roaring ice of the wind, Shepherd stood like a beacon atop the steps of the Citadel and fought for the brothers who'd offered their devotion and the woman whom he loved with every fiber of his being.

He'd felt Claire's panic through the pair-bond for hours, and ached that he could not comfort what he knew must have been frightening for his mate. She was calling for him through their link so loudly that Shepherd was almost certain he could hear her voice caught in the shrieking gale. More than once it had stolen his focus, but he had persevered in his duty.

The hours defending the Citadel were hard fought, but they had survived the siege through almost one day.

Looking at the battle below, Shepherd knew his men would not make it one more. There were millions tearing at the barricades, hastily constructing rudimentary brigades to reach the Follower's sanctuary. Some had even begun attempting climbing the sides of the Citadel with ropes flung over anything that might hold the weight of a man.

There were too many.

His men were outnumbered, and though those who stood by him had superior weapons, the savages below with their kitchen knives and swinging pipes no longer seemed to care if they lived or died.

The herd was slowly breaking through the barricades, using the dead as shields as they crept closer by the minute.

There were not enough bullets, not enough men, to take them all down.

Sooner rather than later, it would all be over.

Shepherd took a deep breath and took his eyes away from the line of filthy citizens rushing his gates, turning his attention to Claire's sky. It was a beautiful sunset, a small flurry of snow falling lightly. His mate would have enjoyed such a glorious view. He would have enjoyed standing next to her while she looked at it.

It pained him greatly that she was so distraught. Longing to feel her comforted, he tried to send her love and reassurance through their bond, a thing he had done for hours.

Shepherd wanted to give her more. But he could not.

All he could do was punish the city for ruining their future and forcing him to leave his mate and child alone in the world. All he could do was take Svana from the city she wished to rule.

He would break any who made it up the steps with his bare hands, watch them bleed, and smile.

Then he would unleash the virus and die for Claire.

The grand doors of the Citadel wide open at his back, Thólos in shambles at his feet, Shepherd tensed at the sound of running feet behind him.

Breathless from running, a Follower rushed towards him. “Svana has been collected.”

Shepherd almost closed his eyes when a wave of warm relief ran over his flesh. At last. “Report.”

“She’s dead. Jules dumped her body on the transport’s gangway and told us to pack it on ice immediately. He took a med-kit from the ship, sir, and abandoned his post.”

Shepherd had no words to match the look of incredulity that blazed in his eyes. “Where is he now?”

The Follower was grim, shaking his head. “Unaccounted for, sir.”

Shepherd's lashes flared, the Alpha glaring. "How long before that ship can be in the air?"

"The engines are cycling now. Five minutes to launch."

They might not have five minutes if the rumbling Shepherd could feel vibrating from the Citadel's dirty marble floors was any indication. Too many raged outside. There was a finite number of bullets available, and it was only a matter of time before one of Svana's bombers crept near enough to detonate. If the building was brought down before the ship was airborne, everything would be lost. "Forgo system checks. Launch immediately."

The order was given just as the building lurched. Segments of the north ramparts began to crumble, one side of the Citadel folding in on itself. Another bomb detonated, Shepherd was thrown, a wall breaking his body's trajectory and breaking his bones.

Hours had passed since it had begun, hours in which sedation that had been a blessing dulling her panic and pain began to fade. Now that Claire dimly recognized all that had been done, she was far beyond screaming.

She no longer remembered their faces, only told them apart by the way they made her body jerk when they raped her.

Hard and fast, he was the one inside her when her child began to die, when the real blood began to flow... and he had howled like a wolf as if the gush of red fluid easing his way inside her body had pleased him. Then there was short and twitchy, he was the one who rode her the most violently, clawing his nails into her skin, marking her with little bleeding puncture wounds shaped like crescent moons.

Half aware, reeling from another blow when she refused to part her lips for the filthy cock held to her face, Claire blinked gummily and heard it again—the Undercroft prisoners were screaming for her in the halls.

She'd thrown up three times, vomited all the semen they'd shot down her throat each time one of them fucked her mouth and forced her to swallow as she choked on the gushes. She was still lying in it, face down, and it was cold, and pink. Sometimes she cried for Shepherd, when she grew lucid enough to feel the pain. Mostly she just stared at the cell's only door, watching the feet of monsters shuffle by in their rags, terrified they would turn their attention on her and reach through the bars.

One swollen eye went wide when the third of the Alphas pulled her hair so hard her head was forced back. She heard him grunt savagely, knew him from the others by the way he liked to grope her when he rutted, and felt him knot amidst the bleeding wreckage of her body. There was no sound from her throat, only a strange echo that seemed to seep from a place far away.

"We agreed no knotting!" A growled complaint was flung at the man with his head thrown back, too busy moaning at the ceiling to pay any attention. "It was my turn next, and now you got the cunt stuck on you cock. Pull out!"

The only answer was a low phlegmy moan, the sound more animal than man. A sharp series of tugs shook the knotted pair, one of the men trying to yank the bastard away. It was useless, his knot was locked behind her pubic bone, but it woke Claire from her stupor, encouraged a shrill stab of horrific pain, and though it had been hours since she'd been able to manage it, Claire found another scream. The high-pitched shriek and the sobs that followed were wretched, a thing full of hopelessness and pain.

"Don't kill her yet, cocksucker. I want this piece to last longer than the last ones." It was the one who had laughed when her miscarriage began, the cruelest of her assailants who warned. "You'll just have to wait it out."

"What's that noise?" the man who had been trying to pry short-and-twitchy off let go, and moved to the door. “Get the bitch to stop screaming!”

But they couldn’t, she screamed and screamed, no longer human, staring out through the bars as more of those tattered legs came into view, certain the Undercroft demons had come for her.

Claire’s arms stretched until her joints began to burn, she fought the binding again when the monster outside paused and grabbed the cell door in an attempt to force it open. A ragged face appeared, but where she had been expecting lips pulled back to show sharp teeth, what looked back at her was outrageous fury and wide eyed concern.

It was just like Shepherd’s story, the shadow ripped the bars straight out of the rock to come inside her cell. A demon had come to claim her for itself. The noise of her attackers’ panic echoed off the walls. There were grunts and screaming. Like magic, the knot inside her shrunk, and the invading painful thing was pulled out. Another wave of blood gushed from her in its wake.

There was a roar of noise. A great beast stood over her. The rope was cut, gentle hands turned her over in the pool of vileness. She could hardly see, couldn’t understand why she was being lifted from the bed.

The three men who had used her lay naked and blood smeared, sprawled on the floor where they’d fallen.

"My name is Brigadier Dane." The Enforcer touching her was female, her eyes determined and shaken as she covered Claire's nakedness with the Omega's discarded coat. "You're safe now, Miss O'Donnell."

Chapter 13

There was so much blood, Claire clung to the woman with the soft eyes, the one who had come to save take her from the pool of pain and take her out of that cage. She only had the jacket and her long hair to cover her, but once they were clear of the tunnels, the Enforcer tried to wipe her down with her own shirt, cleaning the wounds as best she could, while Claire leaned against the wall in a stupor and felt more of her insides slip out.

"They killed my son," that was all she could manage, confused and unsure where she was.

"You are miscarrying." The older woman nodded sympathetically. "Yes."

The sounds of a battle raged all through the city, and Claire dimly recognized what it must mean. A revolution had begun. That's why strangers were rushing by. That's why the woman had saved her.

It did not fill Claire with the rush it should have, there was too much pain for that. But somewhere past the shock she knew, though her life was over, at least a few would be redeemed.

Under the support of Brigadier Dane's arms, Claire tried to walk through the heaving crowds. Her savior was shouting over the mob, calling for a medic, a doctor, anyone who might staunch the Omega's wounds.

Claire was bleeding to death—no amount of makeshift bandages and encouraging words from a stranger would change that. Nothing would bring back the son that had been ripped out of her womb. All that was left was to die with her mate.

The instant the woman turned her back to dig though the nearest dwelling for some supplies, Claire found the strength to get up from where she had been placed. On the cusp of unconsciousness, her legs did not want to work, fresh blood was running down her thigh, but Claire forced herself out the door, shuffling through the streets, a trail of red drops speckling the ground behind her.

It was like moving through a dream, climbing upward towards the light. What remained of the Citadel was shockingly close, Svana having arranged her torture near the very place Claire had been forced to call home.

The war, the rebels, they were right in front of her, all around her. Gunfire, explosions, screams, but all she could feel was Shepherd. He'd been right there the whole time.

She walked as steady as she could, but tripped over the mangled body of one of Shepherd's Followers. The cracked marble steps, those same steps she'd walked up the day she met Shepherd, were only across one last barrier. She opened her eyes, realizing she had almost fallen asleep, and knew all she had to do was crawl through the field of corpses and pull herself up to where she felt her mate's great pain.

That was what gave her the strength to move again, to crawl forward even as the ground shook, and huge chunks of the Citadel began to fall off.

None of it mattered. There was only time for Shepherd.

Claire continued forward.

Her love was so close, and there were only a few more stairs to manage. Claire pulled herself up that last step, resting against the nearest pillar to catch her breath.

Her vision swam just as another corner of the Citadel began to crumble.

The great door was before her. Claire shuffled through blood and glass, finding her legs again, ignoring the way her bare feet felt each shard. And there he was, twenty meters, ten, five...

On his back, still as a corpse, Shepherd lay.

Half-dead, she went to him, saw his silver eyes find hers and fill with horror as he took in what she'd become. All her black hair was matted with blood and fluids, the corners of her mouth torn and crusted. There was so much damage, a river of fresh bright red trickling down her battered legs, smeared from her journey on her thighs.

Falling to her knees at his side, she tried to speak his name, voice hoarse, to call out to the man bleeding and trembling as if trying to move. But he was badly hurt, bright red, seeping from under his charred armor.

There was a noise in his throat, those silver eyes trying to express love past the panic.

Pawing his face, seeing that her fingers were gnarled and swollen, Claire whimpered in grief as she tried to crawl over him. "Svana took our son from my body. She gave me to three monsters, Shepherd."

One large hand twitched, Claire knew he wanted to hold her, but could not. So she lifted it to rest on her hip, splayed over him, pressed to his side where his armor was black and burnt.

She sought comfort from a dying man who could hardly bend his fingers to grip her hip.

Whatever had damaged him, she did not have the power to see. Claire's fading attention found only the wet, silver eyes pleading with her as they grew dim, heard the wrongness of Shepherd's far too spaced apart breaths.

The last of her life drained from between her legs in a pool of red, Claire sagged, her ear above where his heart should have been beating.

Thólos earned its freedom, Shepherd's tyranny ended, and Brigadier Dane wrestled control of the resistance from the few surviving members of Leslie Kantor's rebel contingent.

With no one willing to share the true story behind the uprising, unfitting as it was, it was Dane who was lauded by the public as the hero who'd saved them all.

When a hasty election placed her in the lifetime appointed position as Premier, Corday kept his silence.

What Thólos needed was solidarity, focus. They also needed to come to terms with the fact that despite round the clock cleanup crews picking through the Citadel's rubble, the virus was still unaccounted for.

To survive the cold, the population moved underground, daylight hours barely warm enough to conduct repairs to the Dome's infrastructure and search for necessities.

What happened in the Undercroft, the life of the people forced down there, was not worth speaking of. It was no life at all.

Until the Dome was repaired, there was no other option.

In the months of toil underground, Corday wore the ring, never once slipping the golden band off. He'd developed a nervous habit where he twisted it so hard it bit into the webbing between his fingers. He wanted it to hurt; he would never let himself forget what she'd given, how she'd suffered... how he'd failed her.

Not after the way the masses portrayed Claire O'Donnell as a traitor, not after the government inquest and the amount of times he'd given testimony for the girl on the flyer.

To the public, verbally crucifying a dead Leslie Kantor as a traitor was not enough, confirmation Shepherd had been killed, insufficient. They wanted the culpability of the living. Who better than the dead terrorist's mate, the one found half-dead and draped lovingly over his body.

The Alpha's corpse had been confiscated, she'd been taken away, and each time Corday had fought his way into her sickroom to see her, Claire had been in a coma, surrounded by armed guards, savaged and only breathing by ventilator.

Standing as Premier, Dane extolled Claire's vital role in the resistance, advocating for the woman as much as she reasonably could without inviting riots. As the weeks carried on and survivors began to slowly recover, more stepped forward to speak for her. Strangers holding her flyer testified that she'd been their inspiration, claimed the Omega had offered her strength for the entire city.

That did not stop Premier Dane's soldiers from taking her away.

Dane refused to speak with him on the matter. It took Corday six months to find what they had done with her, petitioning any member of the hastily scraped together government who would listen, demanding to see his friend. He stirred up trouble until the Premier had to assure the torn public that Claire O'Donnell, war criminal, was not being mistreated.

But Corday was about to judge that with his own eyes.

The location of her imprisonment was classified, yet there Corday waited, Dane at his side in the only place under the Dome that was still warm. There were manicured lawns and stunning architecture, a quiet corner of the only functioning region above ground crafted into Claire's new prison.

It was a location Corday knew.

All this time, Dane had kept Claire in the Premier's Sector, out of the grime of the Undercroft, and hidden away where no one could touch her. And not only her, but many Omegas who would never survive the close, dirty quarters trapped with the masses underground.

The North Wing's barred doors were pulled open, and inside Corday saw a place of beauty. There were so many windows that light drenched everything, and though there were armed guards, they seemed employed to keep people out, not force them to stay. Everything was clean, the furniture rich, an Alpha doctor stood waiting to escort the Premier and her guest to the Omega.

The man in the white coat glanced suspiciously at the unwanted visitor.

To Corday, the entire thing was awkward, backward.

Her door was a heavy oak thing, carved and weighty on its hinges, the last barrier Corday would have to cross to get to her. Premier Dane unlocked the panel and pushed it in, the robust Alpha female moving before them to announce her arrival in a jovial voice, nothing at all like the tone in which she'd greeted Corday.

"Good afternoon, Miss O'Donnell. An old friend has come to see you."

And then there she was. Sitting in an upholstered chair, her face turned towards the nearest window, looking out at the surrounding greenery and nearby trees. But she did not move, not even a tick, when Corday stepped nearer.

He knelt at her side, looking over her body for some sign of mistreatment or damage. There was no bruising or sign of neglect, but it was clear from the glassy faraway stare in her eyes she was highly sedated, and that alone was very telling.

Taking her hand, Corday called to her. Green eyes shifted so slowly it seemed unnatural.

"What have you done to her?" Corday growled to Dane, refusing to look away before Claire might recognize him.

"Miss O'Donnell is recovering from severe trauma under the best possible care," Premier Dane replied, tone irritated.

Turning his head towards his old comrade, Corday leveled her with a disbelieving snarl, "She is drugged out of her mind. Afraid she was going to tell me something? What is going on here?"

The Beta's voice had risen louder and Claire seemed to wake, if only for a moment. Her little fingers toyed with his ring and she whispered, "This was my mother's."

Corday forced the anger from his face and gave her an encouraging purr. "Yes, Claire, it was."

"I gave it to Corday."

"You did." The Enforcer nodded.

It was as if she could not register the Beta in question was speaking, continuing as if talking to herself. "So he would not forget me. He saved Thólos."

Lightly taking her chin between his forefinger and thumb, Corday lifted her face so she might find his eyes. "I am Corday, Claire. I am here. I came to visit you."

The woman seemed as if she had no idea what was going on, leaning closer as if to share a secret. "I still hear him you know, purring in the room with me. Sometimes I feel him stroke my hair."

Corday fought not to draw back in disgust, not to let his eyes widen even fractionally. In a gentle voice he explained, squeezing her hand as he smiled, “Shepherd is dead, Claire. You don’t have to be afraid of him anymore.”

“I want to go outside.”

It was the doctor lingering back by the door who spoke. “That can be arranged at once, Miss O’Donnell.”

It seemed a small army of nurses appeared from nowhere, and the woman, the inmate, was granted exactly what she asked for. The French doors overlooking the private lawn were unlocked, a small patio table and chairs exposed. Yet the strangeness of the prison was apparent to Corday, the thickness of the glass, the fact the exterior doors were made of dense metal and not wood, that they had been painted white to seem inviting and not vault-like, didn’t add up.

Claire was raised from her chair, the soft green of her dress settling around her legs. Her doctor took her into the sun. In the midst of the commotion of white coats and guards, Corday wandered about her room, the natural appearance of it, finding nothing clinical. He would have thought it was all a sham if not for the watercolors littering the blue walls.

Everything was images of Thólos, the horrors she’d seen, the Da’rin marked body of the tyrant in several of them. Between the finished paintings were dozens that were only a study of silver eyes in every possible expression. Corday was amazed they let her keep such things, all those stark images of Shepherd pinned to the wall as if he were lingering in the room. There was even a portrait of the man practically smiling, a thing Corday stood before, intently studying.

The paper was crinkled, you could see where it had been folded over itself. It was also bloodstained.

Corday reached up and plucked it from the wall, knowing it was a memento from the siege. He did not know what possessed him to turn it over, but he found a note scratched on the back as if written frantically by an author with scant time.

Little one,

I know you understand why I am not with you, even though it may take some time for you to accept. Do not forget that I love you. I love you, Claire O'Donnell, and I know you will be a wonderful mother to our son. I would give my life a thousand times over to assure your security and wellbeing. Knowing how much you dislike when I tell you that I am doing this all for you, I am going to hazard your anger when you read this, and say it again anyway. Everything is for you, my love. Everything I must do.

Promise me that you will tell Collin daily that his father had pride in him, that I loved him.

I will meet death meditating on how I have adored you from the first moment I found your green eyes in the Citadel, redeemed. You were my redeemer. My sky.

Forever,

Shepherd

"I would put that back immediately if I were you." There was a brisk agitated warning in Premier Dane's voice. Even her expression was hostile. "She would be very upset should she see you touching it."

Corday held it up, demanding gruffly, "What the fuck is this?"

It was Dane who took it from Corday's hands and returned the portrait to its prime position on the wall. Dane's eyes that lingered over a smaller painting of a little boy with black hair and silver eyes hanging beside it.

"I tried to warn you." The Premier put an arm around the young Enforcer's shoulder, less an offer of comfort and more a physical assurance he would follow her. "But you never listen. Come, she is waiting for you outside."

It was humid again, light rainfall scenting the air with the smell of earthy grass. Claire liked when the windows fogged. Everything smelled better for one, the room glowed, the white windowpanes translucent, heaven-like.

She liked to picture the room that way sometimes, as if all that moisture might form into a single massive wave to wash her clean. If she wasn't careful with those thoughts sometimes they expanded into dark territory, the city being sucked down into the bottom of an ocean, decimated. The imaginings would be paired with intense anger, a racing heart, and loathing.

Deep down, Claire hated Thólos.

She would dream of it burning, feeling only relief as flames devoured her city, and wake up in tears. Every time it happened, the air would be rich with *his* purr until she was calm again, until she was back in control.

"You have not eaten your lunch, Miss O'Donnell."

Dipping her paintbrush in red, Claire answered without looking away from her work. "I'm not hungry."

Approaching slowly so Claire might not panic, Premier Dane said, "I thought you enjoyed the rain. Yet you are agitated and have not touched your last two meals. Therefore, I do believe now might be the time to discuss what you are afraid of."

Every morning six or seven pills, physical therapy, psychotherapy, group therapy with the other damaged Omegas who dwelled in the house. Then there were the endless injections. Life was always half in a fog, if you could even call what was inside her life. But there was one thing no amount of anti-depressants could alter—the very real fear of the inevitable.

"You have been recovering for eight months and still refuse to participate in group therapy, to share anything with any of your doctors or the staff." The woman lifted a small Chippendale chair from near the dining table and carried it over to where Claire sat at her easel. Sitting back, Dane looked at her painting. "Are you not drowning in the silence?"

Claire turned her face towards the woman, accustomed to her short-cropped silver hair and wire-rimmed glasses. "And what is it you want me to say? I told you, I don't know where the virus is."

"You have been given a dose of heat suppressant daily, but they cannot repress it forever. Estrous is coming, perhaps as soon as the morning, given your current temperature and disposition."

The Omega's lips formed into a line and anger found its way past mind dulling medication—as did a healthy dose of terror.

Premier Dane tried again. "I do believe it would be good for your recovery to engage in sexual activity."

"No."

She had a way with Claire, a skill even her psychiatrist lacked in gentle prompting. "An

Alpha could be chosen for you. Or if you prefer, you can choose from any of the existing staff. Should they agree, of course."

"No."

"Your mate is dead, Miss O'Donnell. No matter the hallucinations or dreams. What you think you feel is not a pair-bond. It is only an echo you are afraid to let go of."

Green eyes went back to the painting of poppies and Claire flatly declined to engage. "Who says I feel anything?"

Moving to the edge of her seat, Premier Dane asked, "Do you not wish to move on in your life? To have children?"

"I had a child. He died."

"Your miscarriage was a terrible ordeal." Dane took her paint brush away and set it aside. "You were raped by three of the castoffs your mate had left lingering in the Undercroft. This went on for many hours and left you scarred physically and emotionally."

"Do you know when I woke up in this place," Claire began, sneering and bitter that there was no trace of the purr in the air. "One of the first things the doctor told me was that he had saved my reproductive organs, as if I should be overjoyed. Tell me, what the fuck is wrong with all of you?"

Dane nodded, her face serene. "You believe you should not have been resuscitated."

Claire said nothing.

"You were given a field blood transfusion. Did you know that?" Premier Dane tapped her knee with her finger, "A Follower bleeding out from many severe wounds gave you the last of his life instead of saving himself. He died next to you, assuring your heart would keep beating until help arrived."

Looking away, riding the wave of drug induced apathy, Claire did her best not to picture Jules, knowing it had to have been him and doubting herself all the same—the Beta would not have done such a foolish thing if they were all going to die in a matter of minutes from the virus. Yet, all in all, when had life really made sense anyway?

Scowling, realizing the Premier had been successful again in making her think of things, Claire let out a breath. "There will be no estrous. Inject me with whatever you have to."

"That is dangerous, Claire."

The use of her first name made the Omega's lips quirk and brought a small trace of amusement into the glassy gaze. "Is it Claire now?"

The older Alpha smiled warmly, like a mother, and leaned back. "I do believe we have reached that point in our association."

"I am not going to call you Martin."

A small frown came to the woman's face, her brows drawn down. "You know my name is Lucile Dane, Miss O'Donnell. Who is Martin?"

Out of nowhere Claire's lower lip began to tremble from the flash of memory. Eyes running over with tears at her slip naming the surrogate Shepherd had chosen for her, Claire whispered, "I want to be left alone now."

Dane stood and put a hand on her shoulder, staying with her and purring through the entirety of the Omega's meltdown, watching the woman press her face into her hands and sob as if the world was ending.

It was Corday's habit to surprise her with paper flowers he'd made himself during his infrequent free hours, pulling them from behind his back as if she did not know they were already there. The act was always matched with a charmingly boyish smile. And then brown eyes would take a few seconds to look her over for marks or signs of unspoken trouble.

Setting aside The Art of War, Claire left her seat at the window and went to greet her friend. "I am amazed you made it. I have been told there is a blizzard in the Dome."

"Yeah, well." He shrugged sheepishly. "It's only a little snow."

Corday had been furious when he arrived two months prior and had been turned away, told by men with machine guns that no one could see patient 142. He'd assumed the worst, and practically charged the North Wing's gates. Alpha guards had forced him off. Biting down on his temper, he had come back in the night, using the ventilation ducts to break in... and found the real reason he'd been denied entry.

She was in estrous, contained to enforce her desire for celibacy. He distanced himself immediately, already far too close to the scent of her slick. Claire had never known he was there, but Corday stayed nearby for the entire three days it took for her to come through the heat... because she was crying, and scared, and he could not bear to leave her.

Twice a day she was attended by her physician, vitals taken, the Omega injected with something she readily offered her arm for each time. The man never touched her inappropriately; he never responded to her scent. Considering Corday had always found Premier Dane to be an absolute shrew, he had to admit, the amount of care she'd guaranteed his friend seemed almost unbelievable.

"You have a grand piano in your room..." Corday gaped, seeing the hulking thing set up in the corner.

Claire chuckled. “Is that what those are called. I just thought it was a fancy new table.” Setting her flowers aside, she moved to the bench and began to play a song that had been popular before the first Dome had been erected.

While she played, he looked over the wall to see what paintings had been removed and replaced. They never discussed it, Corday’s appraisal, but he could read her life on that wall. It was one filled with Shepherd. Many of the most offensive paintings had vanished to be replaced with watercolors of flowers, what looked like the foam of a cappuccino, and a sea of silver eyes.

As always, the bloodstained portrait of the man held a position of honor.

“You know,” Corday spoke over her music, “you’re much more fun to hang out with when you’re not drooling on yourself.”

He heard her laugh and trill the keys in that comic riff old films added after shitty jokes.

It was one of her better days, so Corday chose to take the initiative and slide onto the bench next to her, pretending he didn’t notice when she stiffened at the physical contact and swallowed nervously. When all he did was start to play chopsticks, she loosened up and laughed.

Shoulder to shoulder, they screwed around, banging on her pretty new instrument like misbehaving children until out of the blue, Claire froze. At first, it was as if she was trying to hide that her gaze was darting around to all the shadowed corners. Moments later, she put her hand on his to make him stop with the noise, and closed her eyes.

Scowling, Corday asked, “What are you-”

“Shhhhh,” she hushed him, face serene, softly smiling. Over the next few seconds she seemed to melt, all her tension faded as she breathed slowly and kept her eyes closed.

Corday was angry. “He’s not there, Claire.”

Her dark lashes lifted and she peeked at the man at her side, a little sad, and very lonely. “Yes he is. He *is* there.”

It was not the first time she had done this, and it was so fucking frustrating. How do you compete with a ghost?

“Shepherd is not there!” Corday climbed off the bench to glare down at her. “Do you hear me? Shepherd is dead. He was a monster. He hurt you! He hurt a lot of people! What you think you felt for him was forced by the pair-bond and the baby he drugged you to create. Pure manipulation. You didn’t love him!”

Corday had figured out a long time ago that she’d need time, having sat in the hearings as the government officials pieced together what they had learned from inspecting her cell, her paintings underground, the nature of her rape. There was a reason so few Follower bodies were found. They had used the ancient transport ships docked atop the Citadel. They had abandoned Thólos... Shepherd had tried to get her out of the city. Even the letter on the wall made that clear. It was the only good thing he'd ever done for her, and Shepherd had failed at it. And in the fucked up half-drugged reality the doctors kept her in, his Claire could not see what was right before her, as if she had shifted the blame to that bitch Svana and didn't remember the truth of her history.

Fighting to control his temper, Corday put a hand on her shoulder and turned her to face him, purring as loud as he could to cut through whatever sound her mind was creating. "Claire, I am a living breathing man and I do love you. I would never hurt you. And I am willing to wait for you to get your head together, but you have to open your eyes and accept facts."

A little suspicious, the Omega remained silent, her ears pricked as she listened to the Beta purr. Shepherd's was still louder, it was richer, and it was far more beautiful.

That night after Corday left, Claire lay in her bed in the dark and waited for the phantom hand to touch her hair. Sniffing into her pillow, she felt the throb of the link, the twist that came to warm her insides when she was lonely.

It had been almost a year, and though her body had healed, her spirit was adrift.

Corday was deluding himself; the Beta would never understand. Whatever future he had imagined could never exist. She would rather die than mate another man. And though it had never been officially said to her face, she knew there was no leaving the room and walled garden they kept her in... unless she submitted to another Alpha. This was her prison, why else would the guards walk the halls with assault rifles and every door be locked like a vault? Even her windows were inches thick glass, seemingly unbreakable, probably bulletproof.

She never talked about Shepherd. She never talked about Svana. And only once in those horrible group therapy sessions had she been able to speak about the rape. And she'd spoken, and spoken, and spoken until she was screaming and threw up all over the floor. They had kept her sedated for days afterward. Several times Premier Dane had come to speak with her about the event and Claire refused to even look at the woman. All the Omega had wanted was the noise that wasn't supposed to be there and the dreams that occasionally fought through the drugs where Shepherd held her in their nest, whispering that he loved her.

Though Claire knew it was only the rush of the wind against the side of the Dome, it was as if she could hear him, calling to her. And like she always did, she slipped her toes from the covers and left the warmth of her bed to look out the window, hoping that for once she might actually see the man waiting on the horizon.

The nightgown swished around her legs as she crept to the glass doors to look out at the blizzard on the other side of the Dome, and heard him again, louder.

She was done with this place and hollow echoes, if he was calling her to the storm, that's where she would go.

Claire had seen the code enough times to punch in the correct order of numbers until the mechanical hiss of the lock being thrown met her ears. She went outside, clambered to the highest point of the Dome she could reach, needing to stand in the wind, to hear *little one* once more.

The blasting cold on her face as she wandered through the ripping gale, climbing towards the source of that call, rushing through the driving snow, ignoring the sting of her feet.

He was there.

Claire could see him, blurry, standing like a mountain, the golden thread between them singing, chiming with each nearer step. All she had to do was climb over the side of the safety rail and take the hand he offered.

So she did.

Violent wind whipped her hair around, she ignored it. She ignored everything.

He was so close, and the glow of his eyes was full of pleasure to see her. It was so loud in the storm, like thunder and pounding of a beast's heart, but Claire smiled and never wavered in her purpose. Not even when the bitter cold waved around her and began to leach away her strength. So long as she could see those smiling eyes, the fact she was falling was meaningless. Because his arms were around her and the sharp needles of pain seemed to drain away until only black warmth remained.

Epilogue

It was a small service, closed to the public and attended by less than six people. Nona French gave the eulogy, the homilies were lovely, and the people who actually cared about her, devastated.

It had been an absolute nightmare for Corday. He sat there, the Premier in the seat beside him, and glared at the empty coffin while he worked his jaw.

The date of Claire O'Donnell's death had been two weeks prior, but the fucking North Wing doctors would not release the body. He had screamed, railed, threatened to bring the wrath of god down if they did not hand her over. Yet they continued to claim that her plummet off the crossing had left the body in pieces, so they delivered ashes in place of a corpse.

Corday had absolutely lost it.

Omegas were supposed to return to the earth, the death ritual burial... Dane's bastards had desecrated her.

When word traveled between the wretches subsisting underground that the infamous Claire O'Donnell had killed herself, she was suddenly a saint in their eyes. It was sickening. Those same people had treated her name like a curse, had blamed her for their suffering after Thólos's liberation. Now the tragedy of her suicide opened their eyes?

People were disgusting.

On the dank walls underground, pictures of her were pasted everywhere Corday turned.

The Premier even called a day of mourning, and Thólos had a fucking ten minute moment of silence.

Corday had gone through her loss once when she'd disappeared from the Omega sanctuary. It was nothing to the pain he was in now. Everything had gone wrong; furthermore, the guilt was killing him.

Why had they not given him the body? Was the fall really so bad she was totally unrecognizable? Thinking back over the last year, obsessing over every last detail, Corday searched for the thread that would explain away his building feeling of foreboding.

How many times had he sat in the softly colored blue room with her when she had hardly been lucid enough to speak? Why were they constantly sedating her?

Claire had never complained about it... and he wondered if she'd had the mental capacity to understand the extent to which they controlled her. She was just one small Omega the Premier kept sequestered like a pampered pet.

Why had they not pulled the plug when she refused to breathe for weeks after she had been found in the Citadel?

And the doctors had been so possessive of not only her, but of the things Claire kept in her room... like she was some specimen, or experiment, and everyone wanted to see what she would do.

Corday began to have a sinking feeling whatever they had been pumping into her was not for her benefit, but for theirs. That was why they would not release her body—they wanted to poke around inside first, to take her apart.

Did they think she knew where the virus was? Had they been using pharmaceuticals to try and pry it out of her?

Corday had slunk around the building that imprisoned her enough times to know, the North Wing was exactly what it claimed to be: a refuge for Omegas who could not protect themselves had they been forced to live with the masses in the Undercroft. So why had they kept him away? And then why had they suddenly given him carte blanche to visit her? The doctors were aware he was gently courting her. In hindsight it seemed almost as if they encouraged it, even the less than congenial Premier Dane.

He'd always assumed it had been beneficial to her recovery.

But that went back to the original question. If she was recovering, then why was she constantly sedated?

After the funeral, he returned underground. Sitting on a worn chair, tucked into the small stone grotto where he slept, Corday stared into space, distracted by the injustice of the situation.

Something was very wrong. Why did he feel like everyone, including Dane, was lying to him?

He waited until nightfall before sneaking into the Premier's Sector.

He cornered Dane alone in her office, and put a knife to her throat. "What did you do to her?"

Even as he threatened her life, the Alpha had looked somewhat impressed. "You saw for yourself, we were only trying to help Claire."

In the months he'd had access to the Omega, he'd been blinded by his own joy, had stopped asking questions and stirring up the people underground. He could see it now—that's why Dane had let him near her.

He let the blade dig in until a line of blood dripped along the sharp edge. "You've lied to me enough."

"You were the one who unleashed Svana on us, who pointed Shepherd's men at our resistance." Hissing, trying to pull her neck away from the blade, Premier Dane growled, "You cannot be trusted, Corday. Be glad that I let you live, allowed you to continue work as an Enforcer, and that no one knows what your part really was in the suffering of our people."

The words cut him deeper than his knife pricked her throat. "You know the circumstance, the reasons, for why I did what I did."

"Yes." Dane did not say more.

"I want to see pictures of Claire's body. I want proof she's dead."

Continuing to appear unperturbed by Corday's threat, Dane gestured to her desk's COMscreen. "Patient file 142."

Withdrawing the knife, Corday typed in the file name. There was a year's worth of gathered data on Claire: physician notes, photographs of her paintings, a log of her treatment. At the end of it all was a series of disturbing images. The face of the dark-hair corpse had been crushed on impact. It was just gone. Something had darkened her skin to grey, left it blotchy in the places where bone stuck out."

"It took us three days to find where she'd landed in the Lower Reaches. We don't even know how she got out of the North Wing. The only video we have is of her walking down the hallway, alone."

"Why does her skin look like that?"

"The heat of her body melted the sludge just enough that it encapsulated the corpse. Sewage leeched into her, there was some kind of chemical reaction."

Corday cut her a hateful look. "I know you Dane."

A frown defined the wrinkles on her cheek. "I know you do."

It's what she wasn't saying, what she'd never say... because unlike him, Premier Dane knew how to keep her mouth shut.

Since the breech, it had been a hard two years for everyone under the Dome, perhaps even hardest for Dane. Now that she was Premier, she had the responsibility of every person above ground and below. Day in and day out she toiled with her cabinet, organizing repair crews, trying to figure out how to keep livestock and crops alive without sun. Her people were starving, several had gone mad.

It didn't matter that she was warm in the Premier's Dome. The weight of the world was grinding her down. Corday knew it, he didn't judge her for it, but he did hold her accountable for everything concerning Claire.

Dane offered him one small hint. "If I could have unhooked Claire from the ventilator, I would have done it. But, so long as the virus is still unaccounted for, it was not a safe risk to take for the people of Thólos."

Eyes narrowed, Corday stood totally confused. "What?"

"I did everything in my power to keep the Omega safe, well fed, and happy." She wasn't defensive, she wasn't explaining herself to Corday, Dane was merely stating facts.

As if the reason was suddenly obvious, Corday's eyes grew wide. Horrified, the man felt the yet unseen nightmare sink in.

There was only one reason a pragmatic woman like Dane would have done such a thing.

The reports were a lie. Shepherd had never died.

That's why Claire had heard him; that's why they sedated her... and every purr she had imagined had been real, sent from his side of the link to comfort his distressed mate as she recovered.

"Did she kill herself?"

Dane shook her head because the truth was not quite so easy. "She left her room and wandered out into the storm... we found a body."

Heart in his throat, Corday demanded, "WAS IT HERS?"

The greying, exhausted woman only offered a whisper. "All tests were inconclusive. We don't know."

The story of Shepherd and Claire will continue
in Alpha's Control Summer 2017

Addison Cain

Addison L. Cain was born in sunny California, but found herself drawn to dwell in older, history-rich places. Japan, Ireland, Qatar, and now Washington DC, Addison is always on the move, always eager to immerse herself in new cultures and people. Her stories reflect the antiquities she loves: deep and sometimes very dark. Driven to push her characters beyond the pale, Addison's books are not for the faint of heart.

An alumni of California State University Fullerton, she earned a degree in Japanese and spent years in Asia studying indigenous Japanese religion. Primeval forests and worn pathways have led to her obsession with gardening. Her Great Dane approves, loping around the yard and getting into mischief. Unfortunately the cat has to watch from a window, and because Addison is a total sucker for his sad golden eyes, he gets hours of belly rubs and too many treats.

Visit her website here:

http://www.addisonlcain.com

Don't miss these exciting titles by Addison Cain and Blushing Books!

Born to be Bound: Alpha's Claim Book One

Born To Be Broken: Alpha's Claim Book Two

A Trick of the Light

Available Summer 2016:
Reborn: Alpha's Claim Book Three

Alpha Control Book One

~ Coming Soon~

Chapter 1

Mid-morning sun reflected off the glass so sharply, even squinting, my eyes began to water. Gloved hands to the East Sector solar plate, I twisted in my rigging, searching out the perfect angle until light might distort and show me what I needed to see.

Right there... refraction.

Helmut flush with the damaged pane, I traced over the almost imperceptible feather-like cracks marring the clear amorphous metal.

Routine maintenance scans had misclassified why K73-2554's solar collection was malfunctioning. It was not a wiring issue, the pane was about to shatter. Damage of this sort led to serious ruptures, evacuations of sectors, and the potential death of everyone inside.

Speaking evenly, I catalogued all I'd found to the tech team supporting my climb from safe behind the Dome's glass. "Unit 17C to terminal. Pane K73-2554 is damaged beyond original assessment. The structure is badly cracked and will need replacing once fabrication is complete."

There was a hiss of white noise before my tech's radio communication came through. "*Copy, unit 17C. An urgent status notation has been logged into the repair queue. You are granted clearance to patch while we wait for fabrication. Manufacture posts a three hour timeline.*"

According to my oxygen reserves, that would give me just under an hour to complete install. It would be a close call, I would have to regulate my breathing, but it could be done. "Roger that. Commencing emergency repair."

A patch on fissures like these might postpone catastrophic failure... then again it might not. Though I could not see them, someone on the inside of that reflective glass was scrambling to install metal sheet reinforcement even as I reached for the tools at my belt.

The human race had learned long ago, that risks were no longer an option. In order to survive, there had to be layers of safeguards and regulation.

Swaying from my rigging, high above the ground, I tiptoed around the damaged section's frame. With the aid of a heat gun and strong epoxy, I did what I could to reinforce what would ultimately be a fatal crack. It was delicate work that required patience and a light touch. Too much heat, and the whole panel might shatter, too little, and the epoxy would not set. I had to account for the sun, the changing outside temperature. I had to account for that blinding glare I was trained never to turn my head from.

Grunts tasked with the dangerous job of outer Dome repair were *never* to let their eyes wander. The verdant, creeping wilderness could not be a distraction. Staring at the open skyline, the distant tips of a dead, crumbling city's tallest structures were said to encourage mental instability. It endangered all those who relied on us inside to maintain absolute focus.

Those caught looking were grounded and banned from making *the descent* again.

Failure of so grave a nature led to social ostracizing from the very corps one had been raised with, the family one worked with. Peers would find you suspicious; friends would ask you to submit to reassignment.

Never would I risk it.

Being selected for the external repair program had already placed me in a less than favorable light amongst my peers – even if the work I did kept us all alive.

We had all heard the stories of engineering grunts who grew obsessed with what languished outside the Dome. Some even had tried to leave, or purposefully harmed the structure that protected us all. If rumors were true, there was even a growing faction of citizens who quietly questioned if the virus was really a threat.

In the five years I'd routinely made *the descent*, I'd seen things outside the Dome people inside would never lay their eyes upon. I was privy to what my colleagues considered temptation. Once a butterfly alit beside a ventilation duct I was reconstructing piece by piece. The insect had been orange, and spotted, and lightly fluttered its wings as it rested so near, my fingers could almost brush it. I wanted to watch the insect, to marvel at nature as my ancestors must have done before the plague. But it was forbidden.

Before the increase in my heart rate signaled to my tech that I might be breaking protocol, I'd shooed it away. As far as I knew, no soul in the Dome had ever known that for a matter of seconds I understood why some grunts grew obsessed with all that lay outside.

"*Unit 17C, weather forecasting warns an 18 knot gust will arrive from the east in twenty seconds.*"

"Roger."

With trained movement, I reached to the magnetic handholds stored in the utility belt around my bio-suite. Swinging my rigging to the left, they were locked into place on an undamaged panel. By the time the wind rushed past me, I was secure, pressed to the side of the Dome, and safe.

It was the second, undeclared gust five minutes later that was my ruin.

Dangling upside-down from my harness in order to get the best angle on the last portion of my repair, I was slammed into the metal glass so hard I lost my breath. It shattered just like I reported it would, right before I felt a sudden loss of gravity.

My rigging had failed, the snake-like hiss of a cable slipping through my belay loop attachment pulley.

I didn't have time to scream.

Plummeting head first toward the ever encroaching vegetation, my backup catch failed.

I was going to die.

Twisting in the cables as I fell, my bio-suit grew too tight. A sudden force left me in screaming pain; jerked to stillness, my arm was caught, my shoulder joint popped from its socket.

Sounds of misery gurgled in my throat, the smallest of breaths was almost impossible. My vision began to clear and I found the world was still upside down. I had fallen so far, hundreds of meters, that my dangling arm could almost touch the ivy scaling the concrete foundation of my city.

Blood rushed to my head, vision going to a pinpoint.

Amidst the crackling call of my tech for a status update, I found myself distracted. I could see them, diminutive simple flowers, my arm reaching towards their vines as if they were a rope and I might pull myself to safety.

I could smell them...

Tears gathered in the corner of my eyes, hot drips running into my hairline.

"*Unit 17C, your vitals register as erratic and your bio-suit is broadcasting damage to your helmet's visor.*"

I wanted to answer, but I couldn't move my lips. I could not do anything but stare at the nine-petaled flower and try to breathe.

"Report, Brenya!"

Hearing my name, the break in protocol, startled me out of waning consciousness.

One croak, the sound of labored breath, that's all I could offer.

It was as my tech had claimed. More than my body had been damaged, a massive chunk had been knocked from my visor. I had been exposed to open air. I could smell the world, the dirt, my sweat. I could even smell my blood where it trickled from my cheek and into my eye.

"Brenya... you know procedure." There was a hedging desperation my tech tried and failed to keep out of his voice. *"Without a status report, you'll be cut from the rigging. I need you to talk to me."*

I'd miss you too, George...

My stomach rolled and unconsciousness won out.

#

It was dark by the time my swollen eyelids blinked apart. Body rocking in the breeze as if I were a spider at the bottom of its silk, I hung limp. I couldn't see from my right eye, it was too gooey with blood, but if I squinted, I could just make out shapes in the moonlight.

Warm air brushed my cheek.

For the first time in my life I recognized what real weather felt like. It was humid, and soft, and I could even taste it when I swallowed around a fat tongue.

Teeth chattering despite the heat, I got one word past the pressure on my throat. "George...?"

Nothing.

Sweat was in my hair, dripping up my temples. "Thiiis is... this issss Unit 17C. I require assistance." I tried to move my fingers, to see if I might upset my balance and turn my body right-side up. "I'm caught in the rigging and I can't move my left arm."

It was a different voice that cracked through the static. "You suit shows an increase in your body temperature. Exposure to outside contaminants must be considered."

The red consumption?

No...

I'd slipped midday. That infamous disease killed in a matter of hours. It was night now, if I'd been exposed to Red Consumption, I'd already be dead.

Another, blessedly familiar voice interjected. "*Sir, her temps were up prior to the climb. Unit 17C is documented as running hot.*"

Oversight would never believe I was uninfected if my every breath continued to rattle. I had to get myself stable if I wanted to survive. I had to prove I was viable, that I could still serve.

My shoulder ached, I could feel how swollen it was, but in a very unnerving way it didn't *hurt*. With a left arm that would be useless and a right arm caught to my chest, only my legs might set me free. Straightening them was harder than I expected. First my right leg wrapped around the traitorous cable, left leg pushing off from Bernard Dome's foundation.

I unrolled so fast I was in a scramble to find a grip before I fell to my death. Bloated fingers caught air, tore at my suite, and finally, *finally*, my glove found the friction of a sliding rope. Where the strength came from, I could not tell you, but I found myself holding on with one hand so close to the ground, my boots could feel the spongy give of the white flowered ivy's leaves.

The sound of my own heavy breathing echoed through my earpiece, a strained grunt all I could offer the team listening in on the other end. Feet to the wall, I began to climb, one handed, until I found a way to loop my only lifeline back through my harness.

Arm burning, panting in huge gulps of tainted air, I let go. The moment I sat back safely in the harness the strangest thought crossed my mind.

It was jasmine... the white flowers were jasmine.

I'd never smelled anything so beautiful.

"I have reattached and will proceed to the nearest decontamination hatch. Please advise."

No response crackled in my ear.

Over the next several hours, no one helped me scale the Dome - though I made continuous status reports as I crept up the side like a bug.

Oversight was watching. George was silent.

When I finally crested the nearest hatch, I was left waiting for those inside to decide if I might live or die. I was exhausted, and Oversight's accusation was true: I did not feel well.

My left arm hung throbbing at my side and required immediate medical attention. I was thirsty, so very thirsty that my tongue stung even worse that the crusted gash on my cheek.

They left me there until sunrise. Dozing against the hatch, I felt it give, scrambling to my feet as best I could. The mechanized door opened, the first of five decontamination chambers waiting for me.

Had my uniform not been damaged, all I would be required to do was stand on the mark, arms raised and legs spread. Fire would blast the outside of my biosuit, heating me to the point my skin would almost blister underneath. Unfortunately, with my suit damaged and my helmet's visor in shambles, incineration decontamination would kill me.

The room's COM boomed, "*Unit 17C, you are to remove your bio-suite and place it on the mark for incineration.*"

Fumbling with the catches and clasps, leaning against the wall because my legs shook, I pulled off the broken helmet and tossed it where it would be burned to ash. Gloves, boots, the suit, every stitch of my protection I peeled from clammy skin, hissing when my damaged arm refused to budge from where it had swelled in the sleeve.

Tears running down my face, I had to force my arm free, praying to the gods my screams would stay locked behind my lips.

When it was done, I stood in only my sweat soaked underclothes, and the hatch to the world with white scented flowers hermetically sealed. In the next few moments, I would find whether or not this was to be my crematorium.

A click made me jump, set my already racing heart into my throat. The room's only other door, the door that would lead to my potential salvation, swung inward.

The chamber beyond was lit, and there were crates stacked right in the center of the space. While I had been waiting outside, a cot had been set up for me, emergency rations left in a bin.

Once I was sealed in, I was not allowed to leave the cramped room. I did not have a toilet, though when the bio-suit protected scientists charged with observing me came to administer a daily barrage of tests, they took my full bucket and brought me a fresh one.

Beyond the point of embarrassment, I let them poke and prod, take samples and scrapings. If they told me to spit, I spit. If I was ordered to take off my clothing, I stripped at once.

I ate from the supply crate's rations and drank stale water that from emergency pouches older than I was.

I had always been obedient, just as I had always been a dedicated hard worker. Like the other Betas in my unit, I, Brenya Perrin of Palo Corps, was fiercely loyal to Bernard Dome's combined effort of survival and prosperity.

From the best I could reason, I had been in quarantine over two weeks, most of that time spent alone with nothing to do, no one to talk to. The only reason I knew my freedom had been earned was a slight shift in routine - the scientist who'd set my shoulder in place the first day, who'd given me a sling to wear over my underclothes, had returned.

After a thorough exam, he offered me a fresh jumpsuit.

He then notified me that I was to be allowed to vacate the decontamination chambers and rejoin my people. Pride made me smile under the stitches in my cheek. I pulled the zipper up under my chin, eager to go home. Smoothing the tangled bob of dirty hair that lay lank to my jaw, I was careful of my arm in its sling, and walked surrounded by bio-suit clad scientists out to greet my friends.

Clearing the final room, I found no one waited for me - not even George, the tech I had worked with for five years.

It was not until I returned to my bunk at Palo Corps Barracks that word I'd been grounded until further notice arrived. The women I had known since birth, the ones I had been raised with, educated with – the ones I'd played with and thought of as sisters – all one-hundred who shared the room with me kept their distance.

I had never willingly looked at the horizon, I had not studied the shapes of leaves or how the wind moved the trees. It didn't matter. I was counted as one of the tainted.

That first night I cried in my bunk, wishing I had never seen the white flowers or smelled jasmine on the wind.

Every morning when the call was made to rise, I would watch my fellow Beta's climb from their cots and dress in the uniform of our zone. I too wore the grey jumpsuit, I too broke bread in the mess hall with my sisters, but unlike them I no longer had an assigned purpose.

Oversight, it seemed, believed I had nothing to offer to the collective.

After a week living as a borderline pariah, after endless skewed looks and terse answers to my attempted conversation, I found I could no longer choke down my meals. I stopped eating. My head ached, my stomach was always in knots. To prove myself useful, I'd taken to unordered janitorial work. I scrubbed the toilets, the floors, the walls, every surface inside our barracks. When I ran out of things to clean, I walked East Sector looking for debris on the ground.

It was two days of cleaning garbage before I found myself outside the East gates separating the various engineering corps from the techs and central Oversight.

George would help me... it's not like I didn't recognize that he had been the one to save my life. He would help me earn an assignment and end this torment. But I was denied entry. The Alpha guard sneered behind his helmet once I'd been scanned, my rank and designation displayed.

To my shame, I felt my lip shake. "Please."

He looked to my sling, to the gash atop my cheekbone that would scar and remind everyone why my face was marred. My visor had broken, I had breathed contaminated air.

I was infected, even if I was not.

When I continued to stand there, waiting as if he might change his mind, the Alpha guard raised a hand to my damaged shoulder. It was not a gesture of comfort or reassurance. Instead, he used his grip to shove me back. Before citizens free to come and go, before all who kept their distance, I fell. Crying in earnest at this point, I put my hand to my screaming shoulder and cowered.

No one made a move to help me, though I could see a reflection of pity in the expressions of those nearest. When I could not bear the shame another moment, I tucked my feet under my body. I made myself stand no matter how dizzy I'd become. Stumbling step by step, I wandered like a kicked dog in the direction of my barracks.

Halfway through my journey, I was distracted by the sound of running water. Sweat beaded at my temples, I was so hot. Upon seeing the fountain sparkling at the center of East Sector's square, I altered course.

Laziness was frowned upon, but I sat there at the water's edge, taking in the beauty of a precious piece of art installed in the Dome before the gates were sealed. This relic had once sat outside the Place de la Concorde. Who designed it, I could not say. Art history was not emphasized amongst those chosen for engineering education. Just as I could not tell you how old it was or why it was culturally important to our people.

What I could say was that dipping my hand into that cool water, wiping my feverish, face felt more beautiful than the fountain might ever be.

Just as put my lips to that sparkling blue resting in my palm, a roar startled me. Backing away from my perch, my eyes went wide, darting all around the superstructure for a sign of what ogre might have made so terrible a noise.

I heard it again, coming closer.

There was the violent sense of inevitability, the feeling of my impending doom. I could not tell you what came over me, why that noise threw me into such a panic, but I could say that never in my life had I run so fast.

Blood was pounding behind my eyes, my legs were wobbling as if I were under the influence of some unknown drug. I had almost made it to my barracks - where all I wanted was to climb under my blankets and hide.

Almost...

Addison Cain

Addison L. Cain was born in sunny California, but found herself drawn to dwell in older, history-rich places. Japan, Ireland, Qatar, and now Washington DC, Addison is always on the move, always eager to immerse herself in new cultures and people. Her stories reflect the antiquities she loves: deep and sometimes very dark. Driven to push her characters beyond the pale, Addison's books are not for the faint of heart.

An alumni of California State University Fullerton, she earned a degree in Japanese and spent years in Asia studying indigenous Japanese religion. Primeval forests and worn pathways have led to her obsession with gardening. Her Great Dane approves, loping around the yard and getting into mischief. Unfortunately the cat has to watch from a window, and because Addison is a total sucker for his sad golden eyes, he gets hours of belly rubs and too many treats.

Visit her website here:
http://www.addisonlcain.com

Don't miss these titles by Addison Cain!

Alpha's Claim

Born to be Bound

Born To Be Broken

Reborn

~The story of Shepherd and Claire will continue in Alpha's Control, Summer 20~

A Trick of the Light

97627919R00178

Made in the USA
Lexington, KY
31 August 2018